THE CHRONICLES OF

Mad Maxine

THE CHRONICLES OF

Mad Maxine

A novel

JEANNINE MJOSETH

For Steve Hilmy, Marcia Semmes, and Carol Mjoseth who have always been in my corner

THE CHRONICLES OF

Mad Maxine

PROLOGUE

Let her cut you," the Fabulous Moolah said. I tried to make out what she was saying, but the fans drowned her out. She yanked me down to her level and growled, "She's gonna juice you."

Finally, it registered. Moolah wanted me to let my opponent, Mangling Maim, cut my forehead. "It won't hurt," Moolah yelled, grinding her lips against my left ear.

It was after midnight at a gritty Brooklyn sports club, my second match of the day. My legs trembled, but fear and adrenaline kept me upright. I clenched the ropes and leaned hard against the turnbuckle.

"She knows what she's doing," Moolah said, glaring. "Take the fall."

Floodlights blasted me from above as I stepped forward. Moolah snorted impatiently and shoved me into the center of the ring, my neck snapping back. I regained my balance just as Maim, more man than woman, charged from her corner. I stared into her savage eyes, took in her square jaw and steroidal muscles. She slammed into me and shoved me into a tight headlock. I couldn't breathe. I slapped her hip to go easy. She squeezed harder. I slapped again, but still no slack, no air.

Thirty seconds. A minute, maybe more. My vision greyed at the corners. A wave of panic hit: I was blacking out.

With the last of my wits, I leaned in and punched her crotch. My fist skidded across her red nylon bathing suit, barely connecting but it was enough. She loosened her grip and I escaped. I flew back to the turnbuckle. I gulped air and the roar in my ears quieted.

"She's hurting me," I told Moolah. "She's not working, she's shooting." I coughed and whipped my head sideways to spit outside the ring. A bald man in the front row twitched his white loafers out of the way.

"She ain't shooting," Moolah said. "Get through this match and you're one of us. A real lady wrestler. But you gotta let her juice you."

The second bell clanged and Moolah swung me out again. Before I could think, Maim had me in another headlock, tighter than before. I was winding up for another punch when a fingernail scraped my forehead, right below my hairline. Something wet bubbled up, and I realized that it hadn't been a fingernail. Maim had gouged me with a sliver of razor that she had taped to her index finger. I peered through a curtain of red, a bloody Niagara Falls. I wiped at my eyes. I was almost blind. I touched the wound, three inches long and deep. Maim let go and jeered at the screaming crowd. I staggered to my corner, calling for Moolah. No answer.

From ringside, an old boxer I'd chatted up before the match offered me a black bandanna. I wiped my eyes and tied it Rambo-style around my forehead. I hadn't imagined this scene when I signed on to be trained by Moolah. This wasn't fake. This was survival. Moolah had told me to let Maim win, but damned if I'd let that happen now. Heart pounding, I stomped to the center of the ring. Maim was going down.

Chapter 1

THE MOST BASIC MOVE

W e're working on the most basic move today—
bumps," said the big woman dressed in black. She was
older, maybe 40 or 50, with brown bangs that framed dark circles under her eyes. I looked around for Moolah, who I'd
assumed would be training me. Maybe the woman was warming us up and Moolah would arrive later.

"For those starting out," she said, looking at me, "Do a
handstand and let your legs carry you over. Land on your back
with your feet and head off the mat, knees up." To distribute
the impact, we would throw our arms out, hands down, and
slap the mat hard. To get up, we'd cross our ankles and rock
forward to a standing position.

A bare light bulb dangled above six nervous trainees in the
ring. Peeling duct tape curled around the corner turnbuckles.
The wrestling ring, covered in stained canvas patched with
even dirtier pieces of canvas, almost filled the barn next to
Moolah's mansion. A large fan pushed around warm air. The
South Carolina sun blazed; it was already 80 degrees in early
September. In a corner lay a forgotten propane heater shaped
like a canon. Butcher paper blocked the building's single
window and three small panes on the door.

"Make some noise, ladies," the woman in black croaked.

A skinny blond in a neon green leotard and leg warmers volunteered to go first. She flipped over and smacked the mat, light as a French crepe. She hopped up and skipped back to the end of the line. No way it was going to be that easy for me. A chunky woman in a Wayne Newton T-shirt took the next turn and performed a smooth, if graceless, bump.

Then it was my turn. Heart racing, I pitched myself forward into a handstand. I commanded my legs to go over, but they didn't seem attached to my body. My legs were a mile away as if in a funhouse mirror. I collapsed on the mat like a felled Sequoia. Oblivious to my surroundings, I gasped. As soon as I could, I rolled over to the ropes and pulled myself up. I'd done everything wrong. I let my hair fall forward, hiding my face on the walk of shame to the back of the line. I couldn't do it. The blond smiled at me and whispered that our trainer's name was Linda.

Next up was a pudgy young woman who was chewing on a hank of hair. Her phenomenal bosom was falling out of a cut-off t-shirt. It was impossible not to stare at her enormous breasts. Her bump was almost as disastrous as mine. I was secretly relieved that she'd flubbed it.

"How many weeks have you been here, screw-up?" Linda yelled. "I'm talking to you, Brandy. How long have I been showing you how to take a bump?"

"I'm really trying," Brandy whined.

"What did you say? I can't understand you," Linda shouted, sounding like a drill sergeant. "Are you chewing gum? You want to choke to death?" Linda glared at her. The woman, who appeared to be in her teens, swallowed her gum and plodded to the end of the line.

On my next turn, I got a running start into the handstand. I thought the momentum would help, but I just teetered. "Now go over all the way over, holding up your head and spreading out your arms," Linda said, crouching near my head. "Okay," I said as if I understood. I crumpled to the mat again.

Icy dread crystallized under my heart. Fifteen minutes into my first day of training and I thoroughly sucked. The wrestling ring wasn't a giant trampoline as I'd imagined. It was a wide piece of plywood covered in scuzzy canvas. The platform had a tiny bit of spring to it, but not much. Two bad bumps and everything hurt. I don't know how I made it through the rest of the two-hour session.

I slipped out of the ring after practice. Behind me, Linda reminded everyone to be back at 4 p.m. for another two hours of training. I grimaced. I had barely made it through my first practice. How would I survive another?

At my new home, I kicked off my sneakers and walked into the shower fully clothed. I soaped and rinsed my clothes and let them fall to the floor. Hot water pounded my shoulders until it ran cold. I hung my workout clothes on the porch banister. Eyes drooping, I climbed into bed and dropped into a coma.

A knock on my door woke me a couple of hours later. A chunky blond woman in knee-length basketball shorts stood on my porch.

"Hi, I'm Big Job," she said. "I wanted to see how you're getting on." She grinned at me and I couldn't help but smile back. "Actually, I was on my way to see if I could find some-one to help with my hair," she said, shaking a box of blond hair dye.

"Sure, I'll give you a hand. Come on in."

She limped into the room.

"You hurt?" I asked.

"Just a sprain," she said, sitting down hard. The old kitchen chair squeaked from the strain.

I peered at her ankle. A hot red knot pressed against the skin. "I'm not sure that's a sprain," I said. "I've had a lot of them and usually the whole ankle swells up. That looks like something else. A break, maybe?"

"Nah, I'm okay," she said, dismissing my concern. "Got anything to drink?"

I got us some tap water.

I wrapped one of my towels around her broad shoulders and arranged the comb and dye on the table.

"How long have you been here?" I asked, staring down into the mass of dark roots.

"I worked for Moolah before I got married. My husband wanted me home and that was fine for a while," Big Job said. "But I want to get back into the business before I got too old. Moolah wants me to lose some weight so I do a lot of walking around the lake." She recrossed her powerful legs.

"I thought being big was an advantage in wrestling," I said. The sharp odor of the dye stung my eyes and nose.

"It is if you don't work for Moolah," she said. "You'll see when you meet the others. They're all skinny and have long hair. I ain't complaining though. She gives me a break on rent for helping with the new faces."

"New faces?"

"People who are starting out," she said. "Like you."

"Any advice on how to take a bump without killing my-self?" I asked. "I can't seem to get the hang of it."

"Nah, just keep at it. It's the most basic thing. Once you get that down, everything else will come easier."

I applied the smelly goo to her roots.

"So, what's Moolah like?" I asked.

"Some people have a problem with her but she's been real good to me," Big Job said. "You do what she says and you'll get along fine. Just don't cross her. She's not very forgiving. She's in this business to make money, like her name says. Can't blame her. She had less than nothing growing up."

"She's a little scary," I admitted.

"Well, that shows you're paying attention," Big Job said, rising to leave. "I'll rinse it at home. Thanks for the help."

My stomach rumbled. I went to fix a peanut butter sandwich but even reaching for the knife hurt. I gently touched the goose egg forming on the back of my head. My stomach clenched at the thought of two more hours of training.

∞

The afternoon practice was a repeat of the morning. I couldn't do anything right. My elbows stung from smacking the mat. My stomach ached from trying to get up again and again. My neck muscles twinged from trying to hold my head up. I still couldn't take a good bump after an hour. I looked over to see if Linda had noticed, but she'd moved on to teaching the "Flying Mare."

Linda reached back over her right shoulder, grabbed a handful of Blondie's hair, and dropped to her right knee. The trainee stepped off on her right foot and landed with a satisfying thwack. Timing was the key, Linda said. The hair grabber signaled the move with a down-up-down pumping action.

"I want to do that," I said, without thinking.

Linda looked over and shook her head. "You're not learning anything new until you can do a perfect bump every time," she said. "Then you can learn the Flying Mare and all the other moves. One step at a time."

I redoubled my efforts, but I couldn't make it happen no matter how I tried.

Chapter 2

GISELLE AND BRANDY

I was even more discouraged after second practice. I started down the gravel road, thinking "no way." I was halfway home when the blond trainee jogged up.

"Name's Giselle," she said, thrusting out a hand. "Want to come over later? I live over there." She pointed to a pink mobile home near Moolah's mansion.

"Love to," I said. "I'd offer to bring something but I haven't had a chance to get to the store yet."

"Don't worry about it. See you around 8!" she said.

At home, I showered again, popped four aspirin, and inhaled a can of sardines and crackers. Then I fell into another coma.

The alarm clock jolted me awake. I felt like no time had passed. I threw on clean clothes and grabbed my silver flask on the way out the door.

Giselle yelled, "Come on in!" at my knock. We walked through a tiny, screened-in porch that led into a living room. The bosomy teen sprawled on a faded denim couch, a tapestry tiger crouched on the wall behind her.

"This is Brandy," Giselle said, nodding her head to the other trainee. "Help yourself to a beer and grab a glass if you want a shot," she said, pointing to the kitchen. I grabbed a beer and rinsed out a jelly jar that I found in the sink.

Giselle held up the bottle of whiskey, eyebrows raised.

"No thanks. I brought rum," I said, holding up my silver flask. "This is going to taste so good." I grabbed a cushion and a piece of the floor.

"I can't believe how tired I am," I said. "Four hours of practice did me in."

Giselle smiled, "It gets easier. The first few days are the worst. My first practice I tried to take a bump and bit my tongue really hard. I was bleeding like crazy but Linda just made me swallow and take another bump."

"So Linda's training us, not Moolah?" I asked.

"Linda trains the new girls. Moolah doesn't get involved until you're ready for your first match."

"Well, that's kind of shitty," I said. "I paid to be trained by the world-famous Fabulous Moolah."

"That's just the way it is," she said. "I wouldn't say anything about it if I were you."

Brandy gulped a huge shot, slammed her glass down, and glared at me. I couldn't help it. I took the bait.

"How old are you?" I asked.

"None of your damn business," Brandy shot back.

Giselle looked at her with a smile, "Be nice."

Brandy smirked and answered, "Just turned sixteen."

"And your parents actually let you come here?" I asked, incredulous. It was one thing for a 20-something like me to make a potentially stupid, life-changing decision, but she wasn't even old enough to graduate high school.

"It's not like they could stop me," Brandy said. "Anyway, they're not my parents. They're my guardians."

Giselle ripped open a bag of barbecue chips and gave me a "don't ask" look.

"Which house is yours?" I asked Brandy.

"Mine's the one with the Wayne Newton curtains," she said. "My roomie, Wanda, is obsessed."

"Wayne Newton?" I asked, crunching a mouthful of chips.

"Wanda plays his music all the time," Brandy said. "I'm probably the only teenager who knows all the words to "Danke Schoen.""

"Moolah doesn't like Wanda," Giselle added. "She's been training for more than a year and still hasn't had her first match."

"A year?!" I said.

"She's fat and Moolah don't like fat," Brandy said. I gawked at her. Brandy herself was a chubby little dumpling. Maybe her giant bosom balanced out the pudginess. We all threw back another shot and sank into the cushions. My tension dissipated with the beginnings of a buzz.

"So, how'd you end up here?" I asked Brandy.

"I wanted to learn how to wrestle so I hitchhiked here a year ago. Moolah sent me back to those uptight Christian assholes but I ran away again. The third time I showed up, she let me stay. They gave up and paid the training fee," Brandy said.

"How about you," Giselle said. "Why wrestling?"

"Short version or long version?" I said.

"Long version!" they said, plumping the pillows under their heads.

"It started at a kickass biker party in the boonies near Tampa," I said. "My friend Connie and I would have missed the turn if it hadn't been for the bloody pig's head nailed to the tree."

"A pig's head?!" Giselle and Brandy cried in unison. I was transported back to the party.

Chapter 3

KICKASS BIKER PARTY

There it is!" I yelled. Connie jammed on the brakes, tire tracks snaking behind us. She cranked her old truck into reverse and down a dirt road marked on a cocktail napkin. Connie and I had become fast friends at the small community newspaper where we both worked, me as a junior reporter, her on the production side.

At a makeshift parking lot, she wedged us between a fat red truck and a row of chrome-trimmed Harleys. An old farmhouse loomed at the end of a large field. At the other end, black-leather-and-denim clad bikers worshipped at the altar of the red party cup.

We walked toward the horseshoe pits, a half dozen male heads swiveling toward us. I was pretty sure they were tracking me since Connie's a little butterball of a woman, thanks to her prodigious culinary skills. And she'd made no secret of the fact that she prefers women. I myself love male attention and got a happy tingle in my pants that shot up through my breasts, crowning each with a little party hat.

Someone yelled "Pippi!" Joann, a physical therapist friend, was waving her arms like she was parking a plane. We met her on the sidelines.

"Who's winning?" I asked.

"Could be Spider," Joann said, pointing at a lean man who appeared to be made up entirely of legs. His whole look was salvaged from the seventies – the tank top, the short shorts, the long mustache, and crinkly, long hair—but somehow he pulled it off. A slender woman wearing a score of silver bracelets and a leather bikini top cheered him from the sidelines.

"You might as well pick yourself out a comfy chair because you're not getting close on this one, friend," hooted a tattooed onlooker.

I looked over at the keg, thinking how good a cold beer would taste. As if on cue, a beefy boy scout type walked in our direction, hugging an armful of drafts against impressive pecs. I was on the verge of nudging Joann for a good old-fashioned ogle when something told me to shut up. He walked up to us and handed out the beers while Joann introduced him as her new boyfriend, Chuck.

"He's a professional wrestler," she smirked.

I did a double-take. What?

If I'd had any preconceptions about rude and rowdy wrestlers, he quickly overturned them. He was clean-cut and chivalrous. It didn't hurt that he was drop-dead gorgeous, too, his mountainous shoulders and mesa-flat abs testing the limits of his pink polo shirt. Brave color choice, I thought, considering the crowd.

"Pippi? Is that really your name?" he laughed.

"Since I was 10. Pippi Longstocking's my all-time favorite hero."

"And you're really a wrestler?" I said. "So cool!"

I pelted him with questions about his workout regimen and how he'd broken into the business. He folded his arms over his chest so that his biceps bulged. He winked at Joann to let her know he was just being friendly.

"Mom's a wrestler. So's my dad, so I grew up in the business. It seemed a waste not to use their connections," he said. "It's a pretty good deal. I work about 20 minutes a day, not including the time I pump weights."

"Sounds good, sign me up!" I said, joking. "Wait a minute. Did you say your mom's a wrestler?"

My mind buckled. I tried to picture my thin-lipped mother folding her apron and slipping off her beige pumps before climbing neatly into the ring.

"Yep, she's a pistol. You'd love her," he said.

We moseyed over to the arm-wrestling table and decided to take a turn. I'd met Joann on the volleyball court behind the Rose, our favorite dive bar. We recognized in each other a not-too-strict tendency toward athleticism. We agreed that being healthy was important but it didn't mean you couldn't enjoy a beer and a joint now and then. I fired up a skinny spliff of skunk weed.

If you were betting who would win the arm-wrestling match, you would have picked me. At 6'2", I'm about a foot taller than Joann. But she lifts weights and brags about bench-pressing her bodyweight.

We stripped off our outer layers and laughed when we saw that we'd both worn our "We smoke everything" tank tops from Skipper's Smokehouse, another favorite hangout. A door balanced across two sawhorses served as our rickety table. Not the regulation 28 inches, but close enough.

We slid into flimsy lawn chairs and clasped hands, palm-to-palm, with thumb knuckles showing. My forearm and hand were a lot bigger, and an advantage, I hoped. We took deep breaths. Chuck lay his hands on ours and said, "Ready, set, go!"

The doobie had softened the worst of my competitive drive, but it still lay coiled inside like a cobra. I began to pull her hand down to the left side of the table. Joann closed her eyes. I could practically see red-hot power surge through her arm and into her hand. We sat locked for several minutes. I could feel myself starting to weaken. Joann, on the other hand, was rock-solid.

Horseshoe throwers had drifted over to our table. I put everything into my trembling arm. Joann pushed back but I wasn't giving up. I had one more serious push in me.

"Time for Joann to lose," I thought.

"Get the fuck out my face, motherfucker," someone slurred outside the circle of spectators.

Neither of us looked up but I could feel their body heat and the breeze they stirred up.

"Knife!" yelled Chuck. A male form sprawled toward our table. Joann's attention flickered and I slammed her hand down. Someone screamed. I opened my eyes, ready to crow until I saw Joann's ashen face and the knife stuck through her hand. There was an awful silence as we registered what had happened.

"Get a towel!" someone yelled. I tried to stand but got tangled in my chair and landed on my ass.

Chuck squatted next to Joann.

"Honey, let me see how deep it is," he said. The wound was gushing blood.

"Don't move the knife," someone said. "Get her to an emergency room."

Joann tried to stand. Her legs were shaking, her face ghostly white. Chuck helped her up, reaching for the towel that had appeared.

"Emergency room," she said to Chuck.

"I'm coming with you," I said, walking with them to the

car. I held the towel as gently as I could while Joann steadied the blade. Chuck opened the passenger door, eased her inside and jogged around the car.

Meanwhile, self-appointed party cops began tying the culprit to a nearby tree. He flopped bonelessly between them, almost incoherent.

"Make sure they don't hurt that guy," Joann said. "I'm okay."

"Are you kidding me?" I said. "His knife went all the way through."

"Promise me you'll look out for him," she said. Chuck drove off, leaving me behind.

Connie came up behind me. "Poor Joann. She was just minding her own business."

The drunk struggled against his restraints then passed out. He woke briefly when half a dozen bikers expressed their displeasure by peeing all over him. He slurred, "Hey, stop," then passed out again. I figured a little urine never hurt anyone, so I didn't try to intervene.

The adrenaline was receding, leaving me shaky. Connie put her arm around my waist. I took a slug from the flask I always carried. I'd inherited it from my father, along with an unquenchable thirst. I passed the rum to Connie and we were off, partying like warthogs. We ate too much, drank too much, smoked too much dope. Swam naked, found laps to sit on, lips to kiss.

Around two that morning, we hijacked the rocking chairs on the farmhouse porch. Connie had switched to coke but I was still swigging beer. "What a great party," I said, rocking backward.

"Except for Joann getting stabbed," Connie said, rocking forward. I squinted to see if she was being sarcastic.

"Can I crash at your place tonight?" I asked. "I don't think I can make it all the way home."

"Of course." When Connie had rocked herself sober, we made our way to the parking area.

༙༙

I woke late the next morning to light slicing through Venetian blinds. Sheets lay wadded at the end of Connie's couch and I was stuck fast to the shiny black Naugahyde. The couch emitted a sucking sound as I pulled myself loose and blindly felt the floor for my clothes. On a hangover scale, I was at a head-banging eight. Thirst drove me to the kitchen faucet where I drank until I couldn't drink anymore. I washed down four aspirin with black coffee and phoned Joann.

"They cleaned it out and sewed me up," she said. "Six stitches on my palm, six on the back of my hand. I didn't feel anything yesterday, but it aches this morning."

I got light-headed. Gory details make me want to keel over.

"Oh shit, Joann. I'm so sorry," I said.

"Don't worry. I heal really fast," she said. "And Chucky's taking real good care of me."

I sipped coffee and closed my eyes. Connie padded in carrying oranges from her tree. She grabbed an old glass juicer from the top of the fridge and began cutting the fruit.

"Chuck says 'hi'," Joann said.

"Hi back to him," I said.

Connie waved. "Connie says 'hi' too."

"Tell him I dreamt I became a wrestler." Connie's eyes got big and round. I could hear Joann speaking to her boyfriend.

"He says you should go for it. Hold on." More murmuring. "Got a pen? If you're serious he says to give his mom a call."

I scrawled the number, repeating it digit by digit. Connie finished squeezing the oranges and leaned against the counter.

Sunbeams touched her tight black curls. She handed me a glass of juice.

"I like the idea of a job where I get paid to work out every day," I said. "Maybe I could write a book about becoming a wrestler." I could be like my journalism idol, George Plimpton, I mused. An amateur sportsman, he'd dived deep into boxing, golfing, and football and had written books about the experiences.

"You should totally do it," she said, grinning at me. "I know you're into guys, Pippi, so don't take this the wrong way. But as a card-carrying woman who loves women, I, and all the members of my tribe, would definitely buy tickets to watch you wrestle another woman, preferably wearing something tight and short."

I snorted and went to shower off the previous evening's mayhem.

Chapter 4

MEETING MOOLAH

A few months later, I was outside Columbia, trying to find Camp Moolah," I said, checking to see if Giselle and Brandy were still awake.

"Keep going," Giselle said. Brandy nodded and shifted to her side.

"I pulled to the side of the road to check my map," I said. "I thought, 'No way a professional lady wrestlers' school could be stuck in this tidy suburban neighborhood'. I kept going and there it was, Moolah Drive, tucked in among a bunch of single-story ranchers."

I passed through an iron gate and got a better look at the front of the property. A long brick wall circled the perimeter of the estate. A pretty lake, divided in half by a thin asphalt road, shimmered in the middle. Squat buildings, one of which would become my home, pocked the far shore.

On Moolah's driveway, a tiny woman in a stretch pants set down bowls of kibble for a pair of white German Shepherds and a scrawny poodle. Another woman scowled at me over the sky-blue Cadillac she was buffing, dark circles underscoring suspicious eyes. Not the warmest welcome.

Behind this strange duo stood a two-story mansion on the

edge of the lake. On one side, a square patio was set with spindly metal chairs. To the right of the main house loomed a boxy building where I would spend six grueling months developing a whole new relationship with pain.

I shut off my engine and eased my road-weary body upright. I introduced myself to the couple only to be distracted by a petite woman in a sparkly blue top in the doorway behind them. She gave a little hop and waved me over. Though the duo hadn't actually greeted me, I thanked them and turned toward the lady in blue.

"You must be Pippi. I've been expecting you," the woman said. The "you" came out like "yew" in her thick southern accent. She held open the screen door with fingers encrusted with flashy rings. One ring sported a diamond-studded dollar sign, matching a long medallion that swung from her neck and disappeared into deep freckled cleavage. A wall of cheap perfume hit me. It was so strong I could almost taste it.

Was this the Fabulous Moolah? She was so old and small, her face a doodle drawn by a bored teenage girl. Penciled in eyebrows arched over tiny eyes. Lipstick stuck to her front teeth. Her face was a mask of pancake makeup. Full war paint at home? Surely, this was not for my benefit.

"How was your drive, sugar?" she said, looking over my shoulder. With the flick of her finger, she caught the attention of the woman who'd been buffing the caddie.

"Linda, finish the car. Darlene can show our new girl where she'll be staying. I'm going to have a little chat with her first." She gestured me into the house. The tiny woman followed close on my heels.

"Welcome, hon. I'm Moolah but you can call me Lillian if you like. Lillian Ellison." She gestured toward the living room, leading me past collections of angels and owls. Tacky times ten. Heavy red velvet curtains banished the blistering afternoon sun. The air conditioner was on full blast.

She trailed red-tipped nails along the back of a zebra-striped couch and sat in what was obviously her regular seat between two velvet bordello lamps. Two magazines, Better Homes and Gardens and Ringside Wrestling, lay next to an icy drink. She patted the seat next to her.

She took a long sip. "You thirsty?" I shook my head but she ignored me.

"Get this girl a Coke," she called to the diminutive woman in the kitchen. "I know she's thirsty after that long drive." She slung her arm across the back of the couch. "That's Darlene, my damned midget." I held my tongue, uncertain whether this was an endearment or a slur.

The small but muscular woman yanked a can of Coke from the fridge and, before I knew what was happening, threw it at me. Thank the gods for good reflexes. I snatched it from the air right before it smashed into my head. I set the can on the coffee table and carefully popped the top.

"Darlene, dammit," Moolah scolded. "Bring her a glass of ice too. So, are you ready to get started?" She clicked her nails along her glass, an impatient gesture.

"Let's get the money out of the way," she said. "Have you brought me your training fee?" In our telephone conversation, she'd made it clear that she preferred the $1,500 in cash.

I reached into my bag and began pulling out the envelope. I hadn't even gotten it all the way out of my backpack before she snatched it from me.

"Can I get a receipt for that?" I asked.

She smiled and said, "You don't trust me, darling? Sure, I'll write you up a receipt." Darlene, lurking in the kitchen, brought her a pad of paper. While she was writing, my eye snagged on a black-and-white photo of a much younger Moolah bookended by Elvis Presley and someone in a tall white cowboy hat. The men towered over her and she had them both gripped around the waist as if she'd never let them go. She followed my gaze.

"I liked Elvis right fine but Hank Williams, Senior... ?" She paused. "He was my special buddy." She stirred her ice with an index finger and absently licked off the droplets.

"We might have stayed together if he hadn't been such a bad drinker. It's sad really. We could've made beautiful music together," she said, nodding to the guitar case in the corner. "Sometimes, I think if I hadn't gone into wrestling, I'd have been a country 'n western singer." She didn't appear to require a response so I sipped and listened.

"Now, my first husband was a real looker. He had real broad shoulders and a tiny waist, shaped like a V. We got along fine at first, but he wanted me to stay home and be his little wifey. I wanted my own money, so I got into wrestling. That's how I met my second husband, Buddy Lee. You ever heard of him? He was a big-time promoter in Nashville. He gave a lot of people their start. He was into wrestling and then later got into country music. You ever hear of George Strait?" I shook my head. My mom, an Oklahoma native, must've heard too much country music in her youth because she banned it in our home.

"Anyway, me and Buddy got married. Things were pretty good for a while but then I realized that he thought he was smarter than me," Moolah said, a crease deepening between her eyebrows. "He told my girls to dress in short skirts and to scream when his talent entered the arena."

From the kitchen, came the clatter of Darlene slamming the silverware drawer shut.

"I told him, 'Don't mess with my girls'. I know we're married but this is business. I won't have you telling my girls what to do'. He was smoking a cigar when I said that, and he reached over and tapped his ash right there on that coffee table." She ran her index finger over a half-inch scuff in the veneer.

"I saw red when he did that," Moolah said. "I grabbed the telephone and wrapped the cord around his neck three times. And then I pulled on it real hard," she said, miming the action.

"He got real focused when I did that. I told him, 'Listen, you little shit, don't you disrespect me in my own house. I bought and paid for this place with my own money and I won't have some jackass treating me bad in it. Not even the jackass I'm married to'."

"His lips were turning blue when I let go of the cord. I didn't see him for three months after that. And that was just to finish up the divorce."

She sighed. "Men are more trouble than they're worth," she said. "How about you? Did you leave anybody behind in Tampa?"

"Nobody important," I said, flashing on the bearded house painter I'd been seeing. I liked him a lot but not enough to get stuck in some pleasant backwater before I'd become somebody. I knew I'd miss my friends. Connie and I talked every day. Now, I'd have to make do with weekly calls to my running buddy. I hoped she'd find a nice girl to date once I stopped hogging all her time.

Thoughts of Connie reminded me of my first phone conversation with Moolah. She had asked if me if was a lesbian. I just had to ask why.

She shifted in her seat. "Well, I shouldn't tell you this, but I had a couple of my girls get involved last year. They ended up leaving me. I don't care who has sex with who, but I can't afford to lose my girls. It takes too long to break them in," Moolah said. My stomach clenched at the words, "break them in."

"Darlene, get me another Coke," she yelled at her tiny servant.

"How long have you been wrestling?" I tried to change the subject.

"I got started real early in wrestling." Moolah explained that she'd been raised not far from where we were sitting in a whistle stop called Tookiedoo.

"I had 12 older brothers. My poor momma. Can you imagine having that many kids? Anyway, she died when I was eight. Things went downhill after that," she said. "My dad did the best he could but he had his hands full just keeping us fed. Once a year on my birthday, we'd go to the wrestling matches, just me and him. I saw Mildred Burke wrestle and that's when I knew what I wanted to do. You know who she is?"

I shook my head, biting the inside of my cheek.

"You don't know much, do you," she teased. "Well, she was one of the big glamour gals. She was a tiger in the ring, but a lady when she stepped out of the dressing room."

Moolah leaned back and close her eyes.

"That's how it was back in the day and that's how I do it. You've got to look your best outside the ring. Like a movie star, hair done, nice clothes. I like long hair on my girls, so you need to start growing it out." She leaned toward me and ran her fingers through my short hair, a surprisingly intimate gesture. I shivered.

She seemed to lose interest in her story and began massaging the ears of her old poodle, her nails trailing through the sparse fur. Her eyelids drooped and she appeared to fall asleep.

I was wondering if she'd wake back up when Darlene

kicked my foot. "Time to go see your new home," she growled, herding me out of the house. She grabbed a key from a row of hooks near the front door.

Moolah had gotten a great deal on used army barracks from nearby Fort Jackson, Darlene said, on the short ride over the lake road. She tossed me the door key and let the screen door bang shut behind her.

I dropped my duffel bag on the splintery wood floor. The space felt eerily familiar, just like a lot of the military housing we'd lived in before my father climbed the ranks.

I sighed and tried not to think of this as a step backward. This is what I wanted: a life outside the middle-class lockstep of school, work, and death.

Chapter 5

FIRST DAY AT CAMP MOOLAH

I awakened with a jolt and experienced the vertigo of an unfamiliar space. My orange Flokati rug, hairy as a Sasquatch, occupied the space next to my bed. I reached down and touched its rough wool. I reached above my head and ran my fingers across the bindings of my favorite books, now stacked in the headboard bookcase. A pearl-diver painting that I'd discovered in my favorite thrift store leaned against the wall. The Japanese diver stood hand on hip, bare-breasted, and exuding confidence that I sorely needed. These reminders of home restored my balance and I let my head fall back on to the pillows.

When I could no longer ignore my screaming bladder, I headed through the kitchen to the bathroom. A battered dinette table and four scummy splay-legged chairs sat at its center. Gangrenous linoleum curled up at the edges of the room. A stovetop sprinkled with mouse droppings and a foul-smelling fridge completed the scene. I'd do a head-to-toe cleaning on the weekend but, for now, I'd make coffee. My espresso maker extruded a cup of Café Bustelo, to which I added a dollop of sweetened condensed milk and headed for the porch.

Across the lake, Moolah's dogs barked at the sound of my screen door banging shut. I sipped my coffee on the front steps, a breeze ruffling my striped robe. Identical little houses dotted the lakeshore. I imagined in each dwelling a kick-ass lady wrestler or two. The caffeine kicked in and I hopped up to change into workout clothes. I set out on a slow jog, running counter-clockwise.

A pair of tall black jackboots aired on the steps of the house next door. On the clothesline, a red, white, and black Nazi flag wafted grimly. I could feel the blood drain from my face. I took a deep breath and crouched as if tying my shoe. 'It's just a show', I told myself. 'Let it roll off your shoulders.' I looked up from my shoe in time to see the curtains twitch. I jogged on.

Twenty strides along the path was a yard full of cats. Half a dozen scruffy felines hunched over plastic margarine containers filled recently with dry cat food. The stench of cat urine hung above the packed-dirt yard. I slowed to a walk and moved toward the nearest kitty, but it hissed and flattened its ears.

A bramble of blackberries twined across the wide gap between the cathouse and the next dwelling, a cute pink trailer that had climbed straight out of the 1950s. Someone had added a tiny screened-in porch, increasing the living space, but marring the trailer's kitschy curves. Country music blared from open windows. Next to the side of the trailer slumped a baby blue Chevette, a confederate flag air freshener hanging from a rusty review mirror. I jogged along the brick wall past Moolah's manse.

Racks of antlers festooned the walls of the next house. Definitely a gun lover, I thought. Brandy's house was next. Wayne Newton beach towels curtained the front windows. I loped four times around the lake. I didn't see a soul but had the feeling of being watched.

At home, I showered and changed into clean duds. A little

before 8, I crossed the lake road to the workout ring. Butter-flies flapped in my throat above a pounding heart. Several older women, probably in their late twenties, sat on a shaded bench next to Moolah's house. Perched like birds on a telephone wire, they chittered and shot me looks over their coffee cups. Yeah, I'm tall. Get used to it, I thought defiantly. I stood up straight and stuck out my chin—and tripped, arms windmilling as I tried to regain my balance. It was a classic pratfall. I looked like a complete klutz, pretty much the last impression I wanted to give the wrestlers on the bench.

"Oh, she's going to be great in the ring," one of them said. "The next world champeen," another woman guffawed. Blood rushed to my face and roared in my ears. They doubled over with laughter, one of them falling on the ground in a paroxysm of glee. I got my feet back under me and kept walking.

The one silver lining was that the other trainees had crowded into a sliver of shade on the other side of the building where we trained and hadn't seen me make a complete ass out of myself.

Chapter 6

MIASMA OF PAIN

The first week of training dragged, intense pain making each minute seem more like an hour. No matter how determined I began the day, the bump wouldn't come. Each time I threw myself in the air, I tensed, unconsciously trying to protect myself. Linda ordered me to loosen up, saying it would make the bumps easier, but it was as useful as a gynecologist telling me to relax during a Pap smear.

After Friday morning practice, I had a phone installed, one of the few private phones at Camp Moolah, Giselle said. The other girls couldn't afford it. I didn't have a lot of savings, but hearing Connie's voice on our weekly calls was an investment in my sanity. I dialed her at the newspaper. The receptionist, whose voice I didn't recognize, transferred me to the production side of the newspaper. Over industrial clatter, I shouted for Connie. After a long while, she got on the line.

"I couldn't wait until Sunday," I apologized. "Connie ..." I paused trying to find the words. "I'm dying here. I don't know what I'm doing. Everything hurts and I can't do the most basic move. I suck." I said, collapsing on the bed.

"Slow down and take a breath," she said. "Tell me what's been happening, from the beginning."

I told her about the four hours of daily torture spent practicing a single move. "I have to perfect the move before my trainer Linda'll teach me anything else. But I can't do it. It seems simple, but it's not."

I told her about dirty looks from the older girls. "They don't know me but they hate me already," I said in a shaky voice. "I've never done a thing to them."

The printing press clanged in the background. Connie was quiet for a minute. "Maybe they think you'll take matches away from them."

"That's a laugh. The first time I saw them, I almost fell on my face."

She cut me off. "The point is, you don't have to stay. I know for a fact that they haven't filled your job. Pack your car and come home," she said. "You can stay with me until you find your own place. I miss you."

I was so tempted. But I'd blabbed to everyone about becoming a lady wrestler. I'd even written an article for my little newspaper. I'd look like a complete idiot if I gave up. I shook my head.

"Thanks, Connie. That's what I needed to hear," I said. "But I can't give up after a week. That would be pathetic. I'll give it another week. If it isn't any better, I'll come home."

My first week hadn't been all bad, I told her. "I made a couple of friends." I described Giselle and Brandy. In the background, something big crashed, followed by voices raised above the din.

"Crap," she said. "I've got to get going. Look, you're new to all this. Give yourself time."

"Okay, but before you go, how are you?" I said. "You alright?"

She spoke quickly. "It's weird not having you around. I'm

a little lonely, but okay. And, I've got a blind date this weekend."

"A blind date? Good for you!"

"I was thinking about dressing up like a drag king—you know, butching out with some dude clothes and a sock in the crotch. For laughs.

"You'd sure find out if she had a sense of humor," I said. "But you might want to play it straight." I paused and then corrected myself. "Sorry, not straight. You know what I mean. You're fine the way you are. Anyone who doesn't think so isn't worth your time."

"You're saying that because you're my friend," Connie said.

"I'm your friend but it's still true," I said. "What do you know about her?"

"She sounds pretty cool. She's a locksmith, owns her own business. Mostly works on rich people's houses," Connie said.

"She owns her own business? I asked. How old is she?"

"A few years older than us, I think," Connie said.

"So kick-ass," I said. "You've got to remember everything so you can tell me. I know you've got to go. I love you."

"Love you, too," she said. "Hang in there, pussycat."

I hung up and took a long breath. The knot of tension I'd been carrying around dissolved just a little. My best pal was getting on with her life and that's what I needed to do. I took a deep breath and vowed to redouble my efforts. Connie was right. I needed to give myself a break. I hadn't grown up with wrestling. Everything was brand new. I had to toughen up, just like Chuck's mom said.

Chapter 7

A MOM AND A WRESTLER

Chuck's mom had been expecting my call. "If you're free this evening, come on over for a visit," Jessica said.

She didn't need to ask twice. After work, I hopped into my '77 Volare and zipped over to her neat brick house on the outskirts of Tampa. She held open the screen door, her lithe frame silhouetted against the living room. A ceiling fan whirred over a roomful of comfy brown furniture.

"You want some sweet tea? I just made up a batch," she offered. Jessica, an attractive 40ish blonde with long skinny legs, seemed as easy-going as her son, and I immediately felt at home.

While she was in the kitchen, I gravitated to a framed photo of Jessica, Chuck, and a big man who must've been her husband. They were each wearing a championship belt with a buckle as big as a dinner plate.

"Where was this taken?" I asked when she came back in. She picked up the photo with a well-toned arm and peered at the picture.

"That was a few years ago here in Tampa. We had to give the belts back, but we got a nice payout and the photo."

I told her about meeting Chuck at the party with Joann.

"She's a nice girl," Jessica said. "The kind of girl I'd like to see him settle down with."

"They seem to get along really well," I said. "Did he tell you she got stabbed at the party?" I asked. Taken aback, she said no.

"They stitched her up and she said Chuck was taking good care of her," I said.

"I'm surprised Chuck didn't get right into the middle of it and get cut up. That boy has no sense," she said.

"Well, he tried to protect Joann but it happened so fast. The guy who stabbed her was on autopilot, blacked out."

I didn't want to have to defend Chuck, whom I really didn't know, or hear his mom tell me things I'd be obligated to tell Joann, so I changed the subject.

"It really blew my mind when Chuck said you were a wrestler," I said. "Do you mind telling me how you got into the business?" I balanced the dripping glass on my knee. She leaned back in her chair and propped her feet on an ottoman.

"I caught some lady wrestlers on TV and decided that I could do at least as good a job as them," Jessica said. "Boy, was I wrong. It's a whole lot harder than it looks."

She'd connected with a promoter in St. Louis and bugged him for months until he gave her a shot. She refilled our glasses. Her first match, a five-girl battle royal in Lakeland, Florida, left her with a bloody nose and a black eye.

"They threw me out of the ring right after they beat the hell out of me," she said. "After the show, Cowboy Luttrell— he was the big promoter in the territory—came back to the dressing room and asked if I still wanted to wrestle. I was so mad, I said I'd learn how to wrestle or die trying."

"Then what happened?" I asked.

"I went back the next time they were in town," she said.

"One of the gals who'd beat me took pity. She showed me some moves to get me started. I practiced them during my matches."

"Wasn't it kind of dangerous?" I asked.

"A little," she admitted. "In the beginning, I got a few busted ribs, a concussion, and a broken collarbone. But I've been lucky. I've never gotten hurt real bad," she said. I did a double-take to see if she was being sarcastic, but, no. She appeared sincere.

"And I got to travel," she said. "I've been to Japan, Canada, Thailand, Nigeria, and all over the Caribbean."

I had no idea that travel could be part of the wrestling gig. The little fire inside me burned brighter.

"There's a lot to love about wrestling, but it's not an easy life," she said. "If you haven't seen many live matches, you should come judge it for yourself." She invited me to see her wrestle the following weekend at the annual Lion's Club benefit.

Chapter 8

LIONS CLUB MATCH

I was keyed up and excited to see my first live match on Saturday. I arrived early and watched men set up the ring outdoors. After building the platform, they covered it in sheets of plywood. They added a layer of movers' blankets and draped it with a large canvas. Two sets of loose ropes were anchored at turnbuckles covered with crumbling mattress foam.

I sat in the long grass and watched people straggle out to the chairs set up around the ring. A tow-headed boy with a new summer buzz cut came up and told me how he wanted to be a wrestler more than anything. He described what he'd do to the other wrestlers, jabbing and chopping the air with his little fists. Over the next hour, fans in tank tops and shorts trickled in, making their way toward the choicest spots. By 1 p.m., a raucous crowd of all ages, shapes, and sizes surrounded the ring.

The crowd grew louder as the combatants made their way ringside. Jessica wore a red satin jacket, her name emblazoned across the shoulders, fist pumping the air. She scowled and jeered, feinting toward a few of the loudmouths. She'd completely transformed from the easy-going woman who'd hosted me in her home.

"You're a bunch of morons if you think she can beat me," she hollered. "What a bunch of ugly freaks." The crowd backed off for a second, but came back on her twice as loud. She yanked off her jacket and threw it to a rotund ringside assistant a few seconds before the announcer began his introductions.

Annie, her opponent, strutted to the ring, shaking hands and exchanging high fives with a mass of beer-bellied men. The afternoon sun pinged off the shorter woman's sequined white cape.

Annie was clearly the crowd favorite, the good guy.

Jessica leaned over the ropes and shouted at a toothless crone, "You're stupid and you smell bad!"

The old woman shot up out of her folding chair and rasped, "You're going down, whore dog." She jabbed a finger at Jessica, who had already turned her back.

The noise escalated until the ref, wearing a black-and-white shirt, pulled the women into the center of the ring. He knelt in front of them, pantomiming a check of their boots for foreign objects that could be used as weapons. He gave the signal for them to shake hands. Jessica held out her hand but then jerked it over her head, humiliating Annie who stood there with her hand extended. The bell clanged and the ladies started circling each other around the ring. At an unspoken signal, they slammed into each other like a neutron bomb.

Jessica immediately put Annie into an arm lock. Annie grimaced and hollered. She slapped at the restraining hands but couldn't break the hold. Annie reversed the move and put Jessica in the same position. They hung there for a few long minutes, Jessica working to break the hold.

When the ref squatted down to tie his shoe, Jessica took advantage and stomped Annie's instep. From that moment on, Jessica took control of the match. She pulled Annie around by her long brown hair with one hand, and wound up her other fist for a punch to the kisser.

The crowd yelled "no!" but she popped her one anyway. Jessica smashed Annie's forehead down on the turnbuckle, turned her around, and strung her up on the ropes. Jessica laid into her with a series of slaps. Angry red hand marks bloomed on Annie's chest. Jessica pressed her forearm against Annie's throat and pinned her against the corner for what seemed like an eternity. The crowd shouted its outrage.

The ref finally pulled her off and Annie fell to her knees gasping and holding her throat. With her other hand, Annie fended her off in a performance worthy of Sarah Bernhardt. Jessica strutted around the ring, nodding her head, confident that she had overcome her opponent. But the match wasn't over. Jessica charged back to Annie with a series of boot stomps. The crowd went crazy, yelling at the ref to 'do his damn job' while Jessica strutted around the ring and razzed the crowd. I worried that a spectator would jump in the ring to intercede.

The ref went to check on Annie, who had begun to raise her head and peer sideways at the crowd. She was tired but unbeaten. She grabbed the bottom rope and slowly climbed to her feet, as though the act had cost her a great deal. The crowd yelled for her to take Jessica down. Annie looked out at the crowd and seemed to take strength from their encouragement. Oblivious to this exchange, Jessica strutted around the ring, so overconfident that she turned her back on her opponent.

Annie charged her from behind, pulled out her legs while she was still holding the top rope. She let go and landed on her stomach with an audible "oof" and Annie hooked her leg for a quick pin. The ref hit the mat, counting "one, two, three!" Members of the Lion's Club roared their approval. The ref pulled Annie up and held her arm high. Jessica railed at him from the mat and then got up and screamed in his face. But Annie had already left the ring for the clubhouse.

"That was fantastic!" I said when I caught up with them in the ladies restroom. Like a lot of the crowd, I'd believed they were angry and fighting each other. I'd even started rooting for Annie, even though I knew it was all a show.

"Thanks, hon," Jessica said, wiping her face with a towel. "I wish we could've shown you more bumps, but it was a real stiff ring."

I looked at her questioningly.

"A bump is where you fall on your back or front," she clarified. "You can't do it on a ring like this one because it ain't got no give, honey. It don't bounce. That belly bump really stung," she said, rubbing her hipbones.

"One thing I don't get," I said. "How can you throw punches and slaps that look and sound so real, but don't hurt?" She looked over at her so-called opponent and smirked.

"Pippi, I hate to break it to you. But the realer it looks, the more it hurts." She paused. "The question is, are you tough enough?"

"I don't know, but I'd like to give it a try," I said. "Would you train me?"

She gave me an apologetic look. "I don't have a training ring anymore," she said, "but I know someone who might take you on. You ever hear of the Fabulous Moolah?"

Chapter 9

SUNDAY IN COLUMBIA

I almost cried with relief when I found out we didn't have to train on Sundays. One day wasn't enough time to heal my wounds, but it was better than nothing. Plus, I would have a chance to explore Columbia, my new home. I thought about inviting Giselle, but decided to explore the town on my own.

I washed down a couple of aspirin with strong coffee and gingerly slid into the car. Armed with a map and the Yellow Pages, I headed downtown to find a good movie theater, the library, and a Unitarian church. I figured I could maybe make a friend at any one of these places. Without someone outside of Camp Moolah, I just knew I'd eventually tell Giselle that I wanted to write about wrestling. That had been my initial goal, but I hadn't written a single word since arriving. I told myself it was because I was too tired or overwrought. But really, I felt like I would be a betrayal of Giselle's friendship.

I first headed to the city's only art-house theater, the Nickelodeon on Main Street. As I eased into a parking space right in front of the theater, I noticed a skinny guy with a scraggly beard squatting next to a mutt. He looked up and smiled as I got out of the car. A self-administered haircut framed a face of extraordinary sweetness.

"Nice dog." I said, noticing that the dog seemed to be missing a leg.

"Yep. And he's partly blind so he's a one-eyed, three-legged dog," he said, standing up.

"Sounds like a country song," I said, reaching out my hand. "I'm Pippi. Nice to meet you."

"I'm Dave and this is Mack," he said.

"I'm new in town," I said, reaching down to pet the dog. "I'm trying to figure out where everything is. Thought I'd pick up a movie schedule. I absolutely adore movies."

"Me too. I work at Kinko's, so I see them all," he said, nodding to the copy shop next to the theater.

"Cool," I said, my eye caught by the state capitol building. "Is that a confederate flag on top of the dome?"

He winced and cleared his throat. "Yep. It's been up there since before I was born. That's a real sore spot, considering that half the people who live in Columbia are Black."

"That's so gross," I said. "I can't believe that's still happening in 1984."

"We tried to get it removed, but those old white men won't budge. Says it's part of our history. But we'll keep trying," he said. "Well, it was nice to meet you. I've got to open the store."

He ambled toward the copy shop with a slight limp that syncopated nicely with the dog's wobble.

He stopped on the threshold and looked back, "Hey, if you're not busy this afternoon, there's a fish fry later on at GROW. You're welcome to join us. You can meet people."

"Sounds great," I said. "What's GROW?"

"You'll see," he said with a smile and jotted down an address for me.

I grabbed a film schedule and then figured out my route to

the Unitarian church, the next stop on my "cracking Columbia" tour. How lucky to have made a potential friend within
minutes of parking my car, I thought.

Church services began at 11 and I early enough to watch
people file into the brick edifice. I was surprised at how dressed
up they were. Many of the men sported seersucker suits and a
number of the ladies wore broad-brimmed hats. Back home in
Tampa, Unitarian church services were held in a geodesic dome
and everyone wore shorts and flip-flops. Despite the formality,
I felt calmer after spending an hour in the quiet. Afterward,
I joined the congregation for coffee and cookies. The middle-
aged minister welcomed me with a warm handshake.

"You've got to meet Harvey. He leads our youth outreach
activities," the minister told me. He waved over a short,
sandy-haired fellow.

"Harvey, I want you to meet a new face in our community,"
he said. It surprised me to hear him use the term new face,
which I now associated with wrestling thanks to Big Job. "I'll
leave you in Harvey's capable hands," the minister said before
sailing away on a sea of blue-haired matrons.

"What brings you to Columbia?" he asked. He was so short
he stood nose to nipple. But instead of raising his eyes to mine,
he ogled my breasts. I crossed my arms over my chest and he
looked up for the first time.

"I love the South and wanted to do a little exploring," I
said. "And Columbia is beautiful." You can't go wrong telling
someone their hometown is special.

"I guess you've already figured out that it can get pretty hot,
but it's pretty great otherwise," he said.

Two teenage girls passed by giggling and saying, "hi." He
said, "hi" back and looked at his watch.

"Would you like a quick tour?" he asked. "I have to stop

off to get some copies made for the evening service, but I'd be happy to show you around afterward."

"What a nice offer," I said. "Are you getting your copies done at Kinko's?"

"As a matter of fact, I am," he said. I told him about meeting Dave.

"Dave and I go way back," he said, steering me toward the parking lot and a lime green Pacer. It was kind of funny to be in a place so small that people actually knew each other.

The door at Kinko's jingled our arrival and Dave looked up from his book.

"Hey! I wasn't expecting to see you until later," he said to me. Then he saw Harvey behind me.

"Oh, Harvey, huh," he said in a flat tone. I explained about meeting Harvey at church and the tour he offered.

He reached across the counter for Harvey's documents. "Come on back and I'll give you better directions to the fish fry," he said, moving to the back of the store.

I joined him at the copier and he whispered, "Watch out for him. He's kind of slimy, especially toward women." I nodded and returned to the front counter.

"Put it on the church account," Harvey said, grabbing the copies and heading for the door.

"See you later," Dave called.

Harvey passed me an old T-shirt to cover the hot vinyl car seats and cranked up the air conditioner. He wanted to show me the Saluda River, one of the city's three waterways. I was just starting to cool down when we arrived. I followed him on a narrow path through a dense kudzu forest, mopping away rivulets of sweat. The trail widened and Harvey pointed at a giant boulder near the trail.

"That's Sherman's Rock," he said. "That's where the Union

Army camped the night before they torched Columbia during the Civil War."

A little farther past the boulder he pointed to the ruins of an old textile mill.

"Slaves made material for the confederate soldiers' uniforms if you can believe that," he said. "Sherman burned that down too."

We made our way back to the car and drove the short distance to Randolph Cemetery. Headstones jutted above a field of purple asters and yellow buttercups.

"We don't have to get out if you don't want to," he said. "You can pretty much see everything from the car. This place is named for Benjamin Randolph, a Black state senator voted in just after the Civil War. He was only in office a few months before he was killed. No one went to jail."

"So, do people around here still think about the Civil War? I mean, the Civil War was, like, 120 years ago," I said.

"There are people here who still hold a grudge against Yankees. I'm exempt because I'm originally from Texas."

"How's that even possible?"

"Well, if you think about it, that's only a few generations. People around here think if the war hadn't happened, they wouldn't be so, I don't know, broke."

I sat there taking this in. I barely knew my relatives outside my immediate family, so the idea of holding a multi-generational grudge seemed bizarre.

"Hey, let's stop by my apartment for a beer," he said.

We ended up at a nondescript apartment complex with assigned parking spaces. He unlocked his front door and I was hit immediately with the smell of old banana peels, coffee grounds, and skunkweed. A tattered Don Quixote poster clung to the wall. He kicked off his shoes, put

Creedence on his turntable, and grabbed a couple of cold ones.

"Here's to you," he said, clinking my beer can.

He fell onto the sofa and put his bare feet on the coffee table. Fungus yellowed his toenails, adding another malodorous note to the room. I breathed through my mouth.

"This is really nice," he said, sighing and stretching his arm along the back of the couch.

"Better than a poke in the eye," I agreed, ignoring his troll feet. "So how'd you end up here?"

"I studied at the University of South Carolina and ended up staying."

"What did you study?" I asked.

"First, I was into psychology. Then I switched to theology. A friend told me it was a great major for picking up chicks." He laughed at his lame joke.

"I know what we need," he said, hoisting himself off the couch. He brought out a small wooden box filled with a bag of pot and some skinny joints.

He fired a joint, took a deep toke, and passed it over. I took a nice long hit. I hadn't gotten high since leaving Tampa and I'd missed it. A giggly feeling washed over me.

"I have to admit that I'm kind of surprised," I said. "I didn't know youth ministers were allowed to smoke pot and drink."

"I've prayed about it," he said. "As long as I do it in moderation and don't corrupt minors, the good Lord is fine with it."

He slid his arm around my shoulders. I was relaxed and didn't mind. But when he started stroking my neck, I got up to get another beer.

"Hey, relax. Aren't you having a good time?" he said,

approaching me in the kitchen. Though he was six inches shorter, he tried to wrap his arms around my waist and pull me in for a kiss. His breath was rotten.

"Dude, no," I said, pushing him back. He tugged at me and up went my knee to his crotch. This wasn't his first rejection because he knew to shift his body sideways. I reached down and pinched the skin of his inner arm.

"Shit!" he exclaimed. "Let go." But I kept pinching.

"I'll let go as soon as you apologize," I said. "In fact, maybe I'll let your minister know how you treat newcomers."

"I'm sorry, really. I thought you were into it. Sorry," Harvey said.

His voice rose at the end as I twisted the skin one more time.

"You need to fix your radar, buddy," I said. "I accepted your hospitality, but that was all."

He stood there rubbing the bruised place, watching me get ready to leave. On second thought, I grabbed the bag of pot. "I'll be taking this with me," I said.

"Will I see you again, maybe next Sunday?" he asked. How pathetic. Some guys never get the message.

"Doubtful," I said, slamming the door.

I stopped a young woman in the complex parking lot to ask for directions back to the church where I'd parked. It was a billion degrees outside so I walked slowly. Half an hour later, I arrived at the church, red-faced and sweaty. I stowed the pot in the trunk under my spare tire. I checked my watch and found that I had time to hit the library before the fish fry.

The sweet neoclassical library was only a few blocks from the church. In the restroom, I splashed water on my face and finger-combed my hair. I took a few minutes to cool down and gazed around the place. Libraries were my happy place.

With the help of a blue-haired librarian, I got a new library card. I eventually selected a copy of T.C. Boyle's "Water Music". The cover described it as a rollicking adventure of two heroes in the heart of darkest Africa. Sounded perfect. I found a comfy chair and read for an hour until it was time for the fish fry.

The sun had lost some of its sting by the time I left. I was early, as usual, so I parked under a tree in front of the austere two-story cinderblock building. On the outside wall, someone had painted a rainbow mural spelling out GROW aka The Grass Roots Organizing Workshop. I cracked open my book but it was too hot in the car. I made my way to sliding wooden doors thrown open to a large, low-ceilinged room.

On one end, a box of frozen fish melted in a deep sink. Battered armchairs butted up against wooden spool tables. It was at least 10 degrees cooler inside so I sat and began reading. Twenty pages in, I heard heavy footsteps above me. A few minutes later, a hefty fellow with a goatee started pinning up announcements on a bulletin board.

"Hi there," I said. "Dave told me y'all were having a fish fry. I thought I'd come early and give you a hand," I said, nodding toward the box of fish.

"It'll be a while until we get going but you're welcome to chill out. Would you like a beer?" he said. "I'm Merl." He reached into the cooler and pulled out two cold ones.

"What is this place?" I asked.

"You've landed in a nest of radicals," he said, grinning. "We print leaflets, organize protests. That kind of thing."

"Sounds exciting," I said. "I'm new in town, hoping to make some friends."

"I'm sure you will," he said, smiling. "Come on, I'll give you the nickel tour."

He led me up narrow stairs on the outside of the building. Inside, a poster of Che and a ringing phone greeted us.

Merl tripped over a rug remnant and grabbed the handset just in time.

"My people will be in D.C. for the anti-nuke protest. I need a crash pad for five," he said into the phone, kicking the remnant into place.

Looking over his shoulder, I noticed a printing contract.

"Sounds perfect. They all have sleeping bags so all they need is space on a floor," he said. He finalized the arrangements and hung up.

"So how does this work?" I asked. "You're radical revolutionaries but you do work for the state department of transportation?" I nodded at the contract.

"You saw that, did you?" he chuckled. "Even radicals have bills to pay."

We chatted a while and I confided that I had gone to journalism school. I didn't mention the wrestling project. I didn't know if he was trustworthy but I had a good feeling about Merl.

People started trickling in. It was my kind of crowd, the men had long hair and the women wore cut-offs and halter tops. I wanted to be useful so I took a turn at the fryer. Hot oil crackled and spit, freckling my forearms with tiny burns. After an hour, I traded places with Merl and loaded up my plate. The sun was setting as I fell into an old lawn chair behind the building. Dave and his dog Mack sat down on the ground next to me. He dug into a plate of grub.

"Glad you came?" he asked, shoveling slaw into his mouth.

"Yay, really nice people. Thanks for inviting me," I said. "Next thing I need to do is find a job."

Through a big bite, he said, "Well, we're short-staffed at Kinko's, but I've got to warn you, it doesn't pay much."

"That's okay. I don't need much. Could you introduce me

to the manager?" I ruffled Mack's fur. The dog laid his head on my foot.

"Sure. Well, actually, I am one of the managers. Do you know how to make copies?"

"Uh yeah," I responded.

"You're hired."

"You're kidding," I said. "That's fantastic. The only thing is, can I work eleven to three? I've got other fish to fry. No pun intended."

"No problem," he said, taking the last slug of beer. "Come by tomorrow at 11 and I'll introduce you to the big boss. You'll like her."

I sighed. Even though training was a disaster, other parts of this adventure seemed to be working out. Next to me, crickets punctuated an argument that Merl and an older gent were having about composting structures—chicken wire versus wooden pallets. At 10, I heaved myself out of the chair. Minus the Christian dickhead, it had been a pretty good day.

Chapter 10

BREAK-IN

The next morning, I woke rested and ready. As usual, I went straight for my espresso maker but stopped mid-step. Hairs on the back of my neck prickled. Coffee grains littered the counter and one of the chairs wasn't tucked under the kitchen table. Either a long-gone soldier boy haunted this barrack or some punk had let herself into my place. Heart thumping, I remembered my car.

I threw on my robe and ran outside. The trunk lock didn't appear scratched or broken. Slowly, I lifted the trunk lid and felt for my five-hundred-dollar cash stash, my passport, and the purloined pot under the spare tire. Back inside, I checked that the orange rug and the Japanese pearl diver painting were where I'd left them. Then I checked the clothes bureau. My underwear drawer had been mussed and my vibrator now stretched diagonally over my panties. The creep was doing more than sending me a signal, she was flipping me the bird.

But the worst was yet to come. I went to the bathroom for a long morning pee and there in the bottom of the toilet bowl was a tiny dead puppy. Tears filled my eyes. Who would be so cruel? I left the bathroom and caught my breath. There was nothing to do but pull the poor thing out and put him in the freezer for a later burial.

I was nauseous and heartsick but made myself go through the motions of a normal morning. If someone was looking for a reaction, they weren't going to get one from me. I brewed my cup of joe and took it to the front steps as usual. Little signs of life around the lake, someone pulling up a blind, songs from a radio, marked the start of another day. But these normal stirrings didn't comfort me. Who had the key to my home? Sitting there, I realized that it was probably Moolah herself who had ordered someone to go through my things and leave the macabre calling card.

Worry, like fire ants, marched across my torso. Across the lake, Big Job limped along the path. She waved and my tension lessened a tiny bit. I decided to go for a jog. Four loops around the lake, a shower, and I felt a tiny bit better.

I forced the break-in from my mind in order to focus on practice. It started with Wanda's usual admonitions to stretch. I did a few yoga poses while Brandy called her a fat bitch, just like the previous week. Linda shoved through the door and rolled nimbly into the middle of the ring.

"Those of you working on your bumps, take that side of the ring." She pointed to an area closest to the door. "Brandy, Stretch, that means you."

I felt embarrassed to be cut away from the herd, not yet able to master a simple bump. Worse, I'd been paired with Brandy, who persistently pissed Linda off.

We got started on our bumps but, on my third attempt, I bit my tongue. Blood filled my mouth and, without asking permission, I slid out of the ring and out of the building. Leaning over, I spit out a mouthful of saliva and blood. I ran the tip of my finger over the wound. Despair crashed over me. All

I wanted to do was hightail it back to Tampa. I was thinking of heading back home to bed when Brandy came out.

"Linda wants you back inside," she said in her annoying flat voice.

Everyone was gathered around a new girl Linda introduced as Zoey. She was a sturdy woman with curly black hair and a gap between her front teeth. I'd seen her going into Moolah's house last Saturday so I took her for an old face.

"Today, I'm going to teach you holds that you'll use in every match," Linda announced. I glanced at Giselle, who smiled and nodded.

Brandy and I practiced our bumps, both of us eavesdropping on the lesson.

"First, let me show you how it ought to be done. Zoey?" she beckoned.

"Lock my wrist at the neck," Linda said. I'd never heard of a wristlock but it looked painful, as if Zoey was almost breaking her wrist. Linda ducked under Zoey's arms and reversed the move. Zoey swung under Linda's arms and moved away into a standing wrist-lock. Linda was bent over at the waist, her right arm fully extended. Zoey controlled her at the wrist, working the joint in a way that looked particularly painful. They went back and forth, switching between standing wristlocks and neck wristlocks.

"You've got to be gentle doing this," Linda said. "Too much pressure and you'll break her wrist. Partner up and let's walk through it slowly." Giselle and Wanda moved toward each other.

Giselle put Wanda into a wristlock, which looked a little ridiculous since she had to reach up to the taller woman. Wanda grabbed Giselle's hair and Giselle jacked her wrist until Wanda released it. Smooth as butter, Wanda reversed the wristlock. Linda nodded. Zoey paired up with Wanda. Giselle moved toward me.

"You already know this one?" I whispered.

"I learned it the first time around," she said. I wanted to ask her how she reversed the hold, but not with Linda looming. I went back to the Doom of Eternal Bumps.

I was thinking about Giselle's first trip to Camp Moolah when I stepped on my right foot, flipped, and landed with a loud smack. My knees and head were off the mat and my arms outstretched. It hadn't even hurt much. My first good bump. I lay for a moment, memorizing exactly how it had felt.

Part of the trick was not trying so hard, I realized. Everybody had told me to relax, but that always made me more tense. So I tried distracting myself again. I imagined Connie on her first date with the locksmith back in Tampa. Would it be a love match? Would it last long enough for me to meet her? I stepped off my right foot and flipped onto my back. Voila! A second good bump.

Giselle saw what I'd done and gave me a loud "woohoo!" She tugged Linda's arm, who glanced over just as I stepped off into a third pretty bump.

"That's great, Stretch. You can officially do the easiest move," Linda said. "Do it another 500 times so you really remember how."

Her sarcasm rolled off my back. It would've been nice, but I didn't really need her positive fucking feedback. An ember of hope ignited in me. I joined the other trainees, leaving Brandy behind.

Chapter 11

KINKO'S

After practice, I showered and headed downtown for my first shift at Kinko's. For the first hour, I sat on a stool by the counter and watched Dave do his thing. He worked like a short-order cook, but instead of slinging bacon and eggs, he bound thick dissertations and laid out flyers.

Between customers, Dave showed me how to make copies, unjam machines, and restock paper. It was easy enough until the first wave of customers arrived. I looked up from the copy machine and the line was almost out the door. Not unkindly, Dave moved me out of the way. "Watch me," he said. He plowed through orders with perfect efficiency. I handled the easier jobs like restocking paper.

"We get a lot of business from the state legislature, bills to copy and bind. I'll teach you that later," Dave said.

University of South Carolina students also patronized the copy shop. Then there were people with home businesses and rock bands trying to draw audiences. The pace slowed around 3, toward the end of my shift.

"You want to grab a drink after work?" Dave said. "Maybe we could hit happy hour at Group Therapy. It's not too far away," he said. I looked at him, weighing the invitation.

"As friends," he added.

"What's the crowd like?" I asked, riffling a stack of neon orange paper, my favorite.

"It's pretty mellow. Hippies, bikers, frat boys, really every kind of people," Dave said, turning to another customer. It sounded like my kind of place.

I took a raincheck and headed back to camp. Linda demanded I do bumps for an hour, then had me watch the others work on wristlocks and flying mares.

Chapter 12

GISELLE

After second practice, Giselle invited me over for dinner. At 6:30, I grabbed a six-pack and walked over.

I found her in the tiny kitchen preheating the oven. "Frozen pizza okay?" Giselle asked over her shoulder.

"Delish!" I said, popping open a couple of beers. "It's kind of nice hanging out just the two of us. You know, without Brandy."

"She went to the mall with Wanda," Giselle said. "You should cut her some slack. Her mom's a druggie. Left Brandy alone while she turned tricks for drugs, even when she was a baby. That's why she was in foster care."

"That is so heinous," I said. Brandy rubbed me the wrong way most of the time, but it helped to know she had a damn good reason for that chip on her shoulder.

"She hasn't had it easy, that's for sure," Giselle said. "But you can't spend your life blaming people for shit. You've got to get on with it. I should know." She crossed her legs and got comfortable on the couch. I saw my opportunity.

"So, tell me about the first time you came here," I said. Had she ever had the same trouble I'd had just mastering the bump, I wondered.

Without a word, she left the room. Worried that I'd pressed a button, I followed her. She was in the bathroom, already peeing by the time I got there. I turned around to give her privacy.

"It's okay if you don't want to tell me," I said over my shoulder.

"It's a long story," she said. "Needed to pee first."

Back in the living room, I dropped onto the cushions and stretched my aching quadriceps. She was back with a shot of tequila for each of us.

"My mom married Killer Sauvage when I was four," Giselle began. "He was the head of a French-Canadian wrestling family. So I grew up around the business." In addition to her step-dad, there was her Uncle Slayer and her Aunt Dominique.

"They ate, drank, and slept wrestling," she said. "When I turned 15, I told them I wanted to be a lady wrestler. That was a real showdown. They didn't want me going into wrestling and that's all I wanted to do. Dominique did her best to scare me. Bookers don't take women wrestlers seriously," she said. "For them, women are a gimmick, like midget wrestlers."

Her aunt talked about breaking a rib at a match and driving by herself, all night, to the next show. The next day, she wrestled despite the intense pain and possible permanent damage she was causing herself. She told her about the kickbacks and blowjobs some of the promoters expected.

"I wore them down and they finally caved in. At first, they considered training me themselves," Giselle said. "They decided I was too headstrong and shipped me off to Moolah." It made sense at the time, she said. Moolah had trained Dominique and had plenty of work for her wrestlers through WWF.

"I had just turned 16—same age as Brandy—and training was going great. The girls even threw me a birthday party. Moolah showed up and hinted that I'd be getting my first match soon. Told me to come to her house that night," Giselle said, rubbing her forehead.

"Moolah said I would be going out to visit an old friend of hers, a podiatrist from Albuquerque. She said I'd get $500 just for posing in my wrestling gear. I was excited to be making money."

The trip to New Mexico hadn't gone as planned. "The foot doctor met me at the airport in these horrible baby blue polyester pants held up by a white belt," Giselle said. She pulled a comforter around her shoulders.

"He was short, bald and old, around 60," she said. "And the smell. Like he kept his clothes in mothballs and then doused them in cologne. I thought I'd throw up."

"He told me to call him Howie," she said. "Drove me to his house way out in the boonies. It took, like, two hours to get there and by then it was dark."

"We got in the house and he started ordering me around like my dad or something." She started pulling threads from the bottom of her cutoffs, the fringe lengthening strand by strand.

"He showed me to this amazing bedroom. The bed had a pale pink bedspread and a real canopy, which I'd always wanted. A real princess bed. I was so tired all I wanted was to slide under the covers. But before I could sleep, he wanted to take a few pictures. He gave me a one-piece red bathing suit. I had my own boots. He told me to suit up and meet him in the living room."

I stirred uncomfortably.

"It wasn't bad at first. He had professional lights and backdrops. I almost forgot he was there. Then he started telling me to 'make love to the camera' and to tug my top lower in front. I was 16, for god's sake. I was so embarrassed, but I went along with it. Then he said he wanted shots of us together. He ordered me to put him in a headlock."

She took a deep breath and looked at me.

"I haven't told many people about this. Promise you won't say anything."

"Don't tell me if you don't want to," I said. "It's okay."

"I want to. Maybe I'll stop having so many nightmares." Her forehead glistened.

"Before you go on, would you show me a headlock?" I said. "I don't know that one."

She slung her right arm around my neck and locked her hands together. I bent at the waist and held onto her hips.

"So I had him in a headlock the way I have you right now and he tells me to tighten my grip. So, I do. Then he starts wheezing and I loosen my hold. He yells at me to tighten up."

She let go of my head and sat on the edge of the couch.

"While I'm cranking on his neck, I could feel him playing with the bottom of my suit. He's giving me the worst wedgie. Did I mention he was in red wrestling tights? His belly fell out over the waistband. So gross," she said, pulling her knees up to her chest.

"He threw me onto the carpet, sat on me, and pinned my hands above my head. His tiny little boner was poking my stomach." She was speaking into her knees. Her voice muffled and weaker.

"I tried to kick him off like Linda taught us but I couldn't budge him. That made him breathe harder. He started to drool on me, you know, on purpose. Ropy spit right in my eyes. I started screaming." She pulled the afghan tighter.

"At first, he liked me fighting him. But I kept screaming. It was like a switch had flipped inside me. I was sure he was going to rape me," she said, squeezing her eyes shut.

"He told me to shut up, called me a 'fucking whore'," Giselle said. "He slapped my face so hard I literally saw stars.

I couldn't catch my breath. He got off me and I ran to the bedroom. I could hear him talking on the phone to Moolah, yelling at her for sending him a maniac."

The phone was on a really long line, she said, so he brought it to the bedroom and put Moolah on speaker. "She told me to cut the crap and do what he said or she'd kick me out," Giselle said. "I couldn't believe someone I idolized so much would do that. That's when I got mad, told her I was calling my stepdad to let him deal with it. I spent the night in the bathroom with the door locked. I never did get to sleep under the canopy. He didn't say a word on the drive back to the airport the next morning. And he didn't pay me either."

"My stepdad was at Moolah's a couple of days later. He was spitting fire," she said. "Moolah was gone, so he yelled at Darlene and Linda. We packed my stuff and flew home to Canada."

Now, six years later, Giselle was back at Moolah's.

"But why come back?" I asked, incredulous. "How can you trust her?"

She ran her fingers through her curls.

"What makes you think I trust her?"

I blinked.

"It's like this. Moolah has a contract with WWF. It's the biggest territory and getting bigger now that Vince Junior runs the operation. WWF only uses her girls, so I need her to get to the top. But I'll never trust her."

"Aren't there other places you could wrestle?"

"I could work for the Grahams who run Championship Wrestling from Florida. But even in independent territories, she can make trouble. She just tells the booker that you're unreliable or a bad worker."

Giselle went to the kitchen. I heard the fridge door open and the sound of another beer can being opened.

"So, do you think Moolah is still sending girls to the Albuquerque loser?" I asked.

Giselle nodded. "Yeah, one of the newbies just got sent out last week."

I felt dizzy. I wanted some grit in my life but working for a pimp was more than I'd bargained for. Then I remembered the break-in.

"Giselle, I need to tell you something," I said. "Someone broke into my house last night. They went through my drawers and cabinets."

Giselle frowned. "It wouldn't surprise me. Moolah has spies."

"They left a dead puppy in my toilet," I said, grimacing at the memory. "What does that even mean?"

Giselle looked as shocked as I had. "You've got to be really careful," she said slowly. "You have a car and a phone, and now you have a job. She can't control you like she does the others. She's showing you who's boss."

"What do you mean?" I asked.

"Well, most of the girls go into debt to Moolah for rent and grocery money," she said. "They pay her back when she books their matches. She's got them over a barrel. They'll do whatever she says because they owe her."

"So Moolah's running a company town," I said. She squinted at me.

"A company town is a place where everything – houses, grocery stores, gas station – everything is owned by one company. If you work there and go into debt to them, the company owns you."

"Yep, that's it," she said, getting the pizza into the oven. "Pippi, you need some backup. You should make friends with some of the old faces. I'll introduce you to Billie."

Chapter 13

BILLIE

On Saturday night, I went over to Giselle's and a big-boned gal in her late twenties opened the door. A waterfall of shiny, light brown hair glistened in the porch light. I was afraid she was one of the wrestlers who'd seen my pratfall. My cheeks flushed.

She smiled and shook my hand. "I'm Billie," she said.

Giselle was stretched out on the living room floor, a pillow under her head and a bottle by her hand. I stopped by the kitchen to stash the brews I'd brought. "Anyone ready for another one?" I said.

Billie and Giselle raised their hands like grade schoolers with the right answer. Instead of flopping on the floor with them, I pulled a kitchen chair into the living room.

"I was telling Billie about Moolah's spies breaking into your place," Giselle said. My face flushed red. I hated feeling this exposed in front of a stranger.

"Did she tell you about the dead puppy?" I asked. Shaking off the image had been impossible.

Billie nodded. "You've got to understand that's just what Moolah does. She throws you off balance, makes you suspect everyone in camp. It's her way of isolating you. But leaving a dead puppy is evil. It's bad even for her."

"Do you mind if we talk about something else? This is making me depressed," I asked, popping my beer. "Like, how long have you been here?

"On and off for about six years, I guess," Billie said. "I came a few years after high school. But she didn't train me."

"Where'd you grow up?" I asked Billie.

"Take a guess," she drawled, slow and sweet.

"Alabama ... Georgia ... Mississippi?"

She nodded her head.

"Coffeeville, Mississippi, population 900."

"Coffee, yum," I said. "What's it like?"

"It was a nice place to grow up," she said. "But if you want to find good work, you've got to move to Jackson or Biloxi ... somewhere big."

"Your folks still there?"

She nodded. "I see them when I can but I don't get home that often. You?"

"I'm an Army brat," I said. "I'm from nowhere or everywhere." I sipped my beer.

"Where were you born?"

"Germany, in a little town that had an old church built into the side of a mountain," I said.

"Okay, then. Where did you lived the longest?"

"Japan, but I was just a kid," I said. "I remember being in crowded train stations. We never got lost because my dad was at least a head and a half taller than the Japanese and blond."

"You really are from everywhere."

We both smiled. "Or nowhere," I said.

Giselle hoisted herself up and headed to the bathroom. I took advantage of her absence to ask more questions.

"So, how'd you get into wrestling?" I asked.

Billie pushed up her T-shirt sleeve and flexed a bicep big as an armadillo. "I've always been strong and I liked TV wrestling. So I decided, what the hell. Not much to lose." I couldn't resist giving that armadillo a squeeze.

"How about you?" Billie said.

"I'm kind of a show-off. When you're this tall, you have two choices: You can slump and be a wallflower or be loud and proud. Plus, I love dressing up at Halloween and I've always been good at sports, basketball mostly. I swear to god though, training is killing me."

"There'll be a point when everything clicks. Just don't give up," Billie said, crunching through a mouthful of chips.

"That's what someone else said," I replied. "But I'm not so sure."

"Billie knows what she's talking about," Giselle said, standing in the bathroom doorway, wiping her hands on her cutoffs. "She's a world-class heel." I nodded, pretending I understood.

"She draws heat just walking to the ring. She's almost as good as my Aunt Dominique."

I held my breath. Heel? Heat? What was she talking about?

"You have to say that. She's your aunt," Billie said, settling deeper into the couch.

"Dominique's a different kind of heel. When someone gets over on her, she'll pitch a fit like a kid. Jumping up and down, kicking the ropes, yelling. The crowd goes wild hating her. And that makes her do it even more."

"You like being a good guy or a bad guy better?" I asked Billie.

"Babyface is what you call a good guy," Giselle gently corrected me. "Face for short. Heel is the bad guy."

Blood rushed to my face and I prayed they hadn't seen.

"Being a heel is easier," Billie said. "You can tell when you're getting over by how loud the crowd is booing."

She took a long sip of beer and smacked her lips. "I especially like it when they throw their drinks at me. That's when I know I'm doing a really good job." I couldn't tell if she was kidding.

I got up and switched on the oven. After several days of frozen pizza, I'd bought some heat-and-eat fried chicken. While we waited for it to warm up, Giselle asked Billie to show us a new move. We piled furniture against the wall and Billie pulled Giselle into the middle of the room.

"We're going to do a cat fight," Billie said. "Follow my lead."

She grabbed Giselle above the elbows and told her to do the same. Giselle mirrored Billie's movements and they tugged each other back and forth.

"When I fall backward," Billie said. "Pull back on my arms to slow my fall. You follow me down and fall slowly into me. Don't let go no matter what."

In slow motion, Billie started to fall with Giselle resisting her. Billie fell back, pulling Giselle down on top of her. The heftier woman then pushed Giselle to the side and rolled on top. They took turns pulling each other on top and rolling to the side until they bumped into a wall and then rolled back again. It looked exactly like a real catfight even though I knew how they did it.

"I want to try," I said, swapping places with Giselle. It was so fun, we didn't stop until the oven timer dinged. By then, we were sweaty and had worked up an appetite

We dug into a mountain of fried chicken, sitting at the kitchen table with napkins and everything. We were on our second helpings when Brandy came knocking, "Anybody home?"

Ugh, Brandy. I didn't want to share this evening or my chicken with the bratty teen, but I sucked it up for Giselle's sake.

"How'd the shopping go?" Giselle asked her.

"S'alright," Brandy said. "I got some jeans and some shorts." She stood and modeled her short shorts. Pink with tiny blue flowers, the strip of fabric was hardly wider than a belt.

"Linda's going to give you grief, if you wear those to training," Giselle warned.

"If those shorts were any shorter, we'd be able to smell you," said Billie, with a crooked smile. Brandy guffawed, delighted with Billie's attention. Giselle shot Billie a look I couldn't read.

Brandy had a mouthful of chicken when she noticed the empty living room. Of course, then Billie had to teach her to catfight. We kept at it until midnight.

"It looks so damn real," Brandy said. "When's Linda going to start showing us stuff like this? All they have us doing is fucking bumps. Nobody ever talks about how to do a real match."

Billie and Giselle glanced at each other but didn't respond. They'd just finished telling me about the heel and the face and the heat. Why was Brandy on the outside? There were so many rules I didn't understand.

We replaced the furniture and made a date to go out for a drink downtown the next day. Our plans didn't include Brandy who was underage.

"You can slip me in," she wheedled. "There's probably a back door. All you have to do is open it," she said. "I'll be invisible. Pleeeeeease."

Not even Houdini could hide those big boobs, I thought, but didn't say a word. She was Giselle's friend. Let her sort it out.

Chapter 14

BRANDY'S LEG DROP

At practice the next morning, Brandy was in the ring, whispering to Giselle. I could tell she was still trying to talk her into coming to the bar with us. Without thinking, I pretended to trip and stumbled into Giselle. She caught me and we both collapsed laughing in a heap as Linda slid into the ring.

"Brandy, get over here," Linda said, ignoring us as we scrambled up. Brandy did as she was told.

"You're just about useless, but I figured out something you might be able to do," Linda said. "Go to the middle of the ring and lie on your back. Keep your arms at your sides. That's all you have to do."

When Brandy was positioned, Linda launched herself in the air, intending to land with her leg across Brandy's neck. Brandy went wide-eyed and shielded her chest with her arms. I would've done the same.

"You dumb ass," Linda hollered. "I said arms at your sides." Brandy's lower lip trembled.

"We're going do it again and this time do what I tell you," Linda said.

Linda jumped again. She landed and Brandy kept her arms low. Brandy's neck fit exactly into the crook of Linda's leg.

Brandy blinked. "That didn't hurt at all!"

"Of course, it didn't. My knee bends where your neck is. Now you try it on me. And if you hurt me, catch my leg with your neck, you're going to regret it." Linda glared at Brandy.

I stepped forward, surprising myself. "She can try it on me," I said. I was feeling guilty about not taking Brandy with us to the bar.

"Be my guest," Linda said. She moved away and I lay down where Brandy had been. I closed my eyes and held my breath.

Brandy churned her plump little legs, leaped in the air and landed with her knee across my neck. I didn't feel a thing.

"Well, I don't believe it," Linda said. "Something you can actually do right."

Brandy came over, and offered me a hand up, a first.

"Nice one," I whispered. Brandy smiled. We spent the next 20 minutes trading leg drops. By the end, I was dreaming of my first cold beer.

Chapter 15

CAT FIGHT AT GROUP THERAPY

F rat boys with backward baseball caps were shooting pool in Group Therapy when we arrived. Dave's favorite dive was a boring square building made of concrete blocks. Despite its boxy exterior, someone had installed a fancy brass Victorian lady on its threshold. Hundreds of framed photos covered the walls. A bearded bartender, with an unfortunate fat-to-muscle ratio, sidled up.

"Who are they?" I asked, nodding to the pictures.

"People who've needed Group Therapy," he said, chuckling at his own joke. "Mostly, people from around here. Football players. A few celebrities. Some bigwigs like Senator Thurmond." He nodded to a photo of an old man in a dark suit. He swiped at the bar with a dirty rag.

"Tequila shots all around," Giselle said. "Draft chasers."

The bartender focused on her curly blondness. "Cuervo okay?

She leaned over the bar toward him, "That'll do just fine. Mick light for the beer," she said, pointing to the tap. He lined up the shot glasses.

While he served us, Giselle borrowed quarters from Billie and sashayed over to the jukebox. She danced back to her stool to ZZ Top's "Gimme All Your Loving." The place was almost empty so I'm not sure who the wiggle was for.

Squeezing between us, she grabbed a shot glass and toasted, "To lady wrestlers." We clinked glasses, threw back our shots, and reached for our beers. The bar's patrons shifted their attention toward us. They reminded me of zombies who were slowly waking up. A few more customers trickled in. Giselle ordered another round just as "Girls Just Want to Have Fun" came on.

Billie started telling us about wrestling in Japan. She'd been working steadily for a few years and thought she knew what she was doing. She'd been unprepared for the blood-thirsty crowds or getting hurt night after night.

"The Japanese girls are well trained, but they don't pull their punches," Billie said. "Every match is a shoot." I could've listened to her all night, but Giselle was hyper.

"I want to try out the cat fight you showed us," she said, putting her beer mug down with a loud chunk. My stomach lurched. I didn't want to make a spectacle of myself.

"C'mon, Giselle. Can't we just have a few drinks."

They ignored me. Billie yanked Giselle's hair and pulled her head back hard. "Like this?" Billie asked. Giselle grabbed Billie's hair and snarled loud.

The room went still. All eyes were on us, including the bartender's. Mortified and a little excited, I tried to get off my stool. Too late. Billie bent Giselle backward over my lap. Fuck it, I thought. I turned my right hand into a claw, threw it above my head for dramatic effect and plunged it into Giselle's solar plexus. She screamed in mock agony, grabbing my arm.

Giselle pulled me down to the floor, which was covered in cigarette butts. I slowed her fall like Billie had shown us. It wasn't graceful but at least she didn't hit the floor at full speed. I pitched myself to her side and rolled Giselle above me. She pretended to bash my head on the floor. I howled, trying to sell it. We rolled to the far wall and we started moving back to the middle of the room. "You slut!" she shouted. "I told you to keep your hands off my man! I'm going to kill you."

We were getting ready for another sweep of the floor when the bartender tore his eyes away from us and reached for the phone. Billie reached down and snatched us up. She held us apart while we snarled and swiped at each other.

"Stop it," Billie roared. "Right now!"

"Did you see what she did to my hair?" I argued.

"You scratched me!" Giselle yelled. Billie rattled us like maracas and told us to shake hands. We scowled and pretended to resist.

"Shake hands, goddammit!" she barked. We shook hands, still scowling. Slowly, we resumed our seats at the bar.

The bartender still held the phone, shaking his head. "Y'all are welcome here, but I can't have fights. That happens again, I'm calling the cops. I'll have to bar you." He seemed kind of apologetic.

"We're just fooling around," I said. "We're wrestlers."

"That wasn't a for-real fight?" he said, relief replacing a look of concern.

"Nah," I said. "Sorry, it was a spur of the moment idea." Giselle pulled a cigarette butt off my back and flicked it into an ashtray.

"Next time let me know," he said. "The owner'd have a conniption if he saw that."

He refilled our shot glasses and set out one for himself. "On the house," he said. We clinked and threw them back, pleased with ourselves.

He motioned to the wall, "How about bringing in a photo for our wall of fame?"

"We've got to get them taken first, but sure!" Giselle said.

All of a sudden we had a fan club. The frat boys surrounded us along with other patrons who'd seen our performance. Giselle held court, giving a play-by-play of the catfight and talking about training.

At the edge of the circle, a tall man made eye contact with me. He had dark blond hair and glasses. Nerdy, but in a good way. I magnanimously forgave the many pocketed safari jacket he was wearing. Anyone can make a bad fashion choice, I thought.

"You really a wrestler?" he asked.

"Not yet. I'm still in training. Same as her," I said, pointing to Giselle.

"Warrior women are cool," he said. "I'm Keith."

"Warrior what? What do you mean?" I asked, warily. I'd heard about the creepy mouth breathers and hoped he wasn't one of them.

He switched the book he was carrying to his left hand. "You know, comic book superheroes, sci-fi, mythology, like that."

"I haven't read much science fiction, but I loved Greek myths when I was a kid," I said.

Giselle had moved closer to Billie while the scrum of jocks eyed her hungrily. She was playing with Billie's hair, wrapping it around her own head like a turban and nuzzling her neck. The jocks were whispering.

"Have you read "Dune?" He held up the book he'd been reading in the dim light of the bar. "I could lend you my copy when I'm done. Actually, the movie just opened. You wouldn't want to go with me, would you?"

He looked harmless and I wanted to make friends outside of Camp Moolah. "Sure, why not?" I said.

Giselle sidled up as I was scribbling my number on a coaster.

"Okay if we sit in the back seat on the way home?" she asked. She reached across me for her beer mug, sliding her breast across my forearm. She grinned, slammed the last of her beer and skipped back to Billie who was waiting by the door. The guys she'd dazzled called after her but she was gone.

"No problem," I said. "Happy to chauffeur."

I pushed through to the front of the bar and looked back. Keith was standing where I'd left him. He smiled and waved and I waved back.

The catfight had jacked me up and I wanted to talk about it. But Billie and Giselle were squirming around the back seat, oblivious. I cranked up the radio to drown out their giggles.

Chapter 16

MEETING THE NAZI

My bedroom reeked of beer and cigarettes. I lifted my head, hungover and grimacing. I sank back but the stench was overwhelming. I heaved myself out of bed and threw my stinking sheets and clothes on the porch. Time to clean up my act.

In the shower, I opened my mouth to the spray and scrubbed my tongue with a washcloth. Embarrassment crashed over me: the catfight, the jocks, my friends making out. I pushed it from my mind and made an espresso.

I focused on my 'to dos.' Laundry. Groceries. Bury the frozen puppy. Talk to Connie. But first, clean my car. Drunk as they were, Billie and Giselle had bitched about the fast food wrappers they'd had to sweep off the seats. I gathered garbage bags and cleaning supplies and went outside.

I rolled down the car windows, put the key in the ignition and found Elvis Costello on the radio. Humming along, I shoveled the trash into bags and moved on to the car mats. I banged a silty mat against the duplex wall and was reaching for the other when the back of my head prickled. I could feel eyes on me as clearly as if someone was tapping my shoulder. Not only was I hung over and feeling antisocial, I was grimier than usual. I pushed hair out of my eyes with the heel of my hand and turned.

There he was, big and white as a refrigerator. Fist on hips, he had puffed up his chest like a rooster. His bleach blond hair was cut long on top and tight on the sides, a style I'd seen in old World War II movies.

I waited. My grandfather had always said the first to speak was the weakest. I clamped my teeth and let the silence hang. When he didn't speak, I turned back to cleaning my car. He stepped forward with his hand extended.

"Wolfgang Schmitt. I live next door," he said. "Been seeing you around. Thought I'd say hi."

"I'm pretty dirty," I said, raising my hand. He shook it anyway.

"Nice to meet you. Pippi," I said, shaking his hand.

He brightened when I told him I'd lived in Tampa.

"Love working down there. Shot a lot of promos at the Sportatorium," he said. "You know Eddie Graham and his son, Mike? They run Championship Wrestling from Florida. Gordon Solie's a good friend too. I'd be down there if it wasn't for Crystal, but Moolah wants her here."

"Crystal's your girlfriend?" I asked. "I haven't met her yet. I'm just starting out. Don't really know any of the Tampa wrestlers. Is that your home town?"

"Nah, I'm from the Garden State," he said. When I looked perplexed, he added, "New Jersey."

"The pretty part or the part near New York City?"

He laughed. "Cape May, down the shore. Great beaches. When I left home, I moved to Hoboken, right next to Manhattan."

"You see your folks much?" I asked.

"It's 10-hour drive from here so not often," he said. "I visit when I have a shot near there or when I get hurt. Mom's a nurse. She's not crazy about me wrestling."

I slung the rag over my shoulder and leaned against the car door. "Mine too. My mom is sure that I'm going to kill myself. You been injured?"

"Nothing too bad. Concussions, broken ribs," he said. Like Jessica, injuries appeared to be the price of admission.

"Hard core," I said. "Your dad a wrestler?" I asked.

"Nah, he's a firefighter."

"That'd be a good gimmick," I said. "Women love fire-fighters. They're so hunky."

He laughed. "Not my dad. He's shaped like a fireplug. But my mom loves him."

"A firefighter shaped like a fireplug," I said, laughing.

He smiled. "Gotta get going but if you need help with any moves, find me," he said, with a hint of a leer.

"You sure that'd be okay with Crystal?" I asked.

"Don't worry about her," he said. "She'll do what I tell her." His comment left a bad taste in my mouth. I couldn't resist goading him.

"So, what's with the Nazi flag on your clothes line?"

"It's a gimmick," he said, smiling slightly. "I get tons of heat. Heat sells tickets," he said.

"Doesn't it bother you? I mean, the Nazis killed 6 million people."

"Heat is heat," he said. "You'll see." I watched his broad back recede as he walked away.

I finished cleaning the car, yelling at myself for judging what I didn't understand yet. Dread pooled in my stomach. I knew I had to dig a hole and bury the poor little dog. He was so small, it took no time at all. I gently placed his frozen carcass in a grave behind my home and covered him with dirt. I couldn't resist saying a few words. "You were an innocent creature, full of potential and love. This shouldn't have happened to you and I'm sorry. I hope karma kicks the person responsible for your death so hard their teeth fall out. Rest in peace, little one."

I shucked off my duds and threw them in my dirty clothes bag. After showering off the morning's dirt and despair, I turned to my next chore, laundry, which I didn't really mind. I loved the smell of freshly laundered clothes. Watching the clothes toss in merry circles calmed me and I even enjoyed folding them. After my first load, I sat and ticked off the remaining chores. Groceries, then call Connie. I decided not to tell her about the puppy. She would get too upset.

In the Piggly Wiggly, my cart tried to steer itself to the frozen pizza aisle but I navigated it toward healthier options. I loaded up on cans of black beans, yellow rice, ripe plantains, and jalapeños. Then salsa, flour tortillas and sour cream for burritos. Romaine, tomatoes and tomatillos, carrots, cukes, and blue cheese dressing. Finally, chicken quarters and barbecue sauce, a block of cheddar cheese, eggs and saltines. I was in line when I realized I'd forgotten coffee and dashed back while the people behind me grumbled. At home, I inhaled a skillet of cheesy eggs and picked up the phone.

Connie picked up on the third ring. "Hey girl," I said. "It's your long-lost pal." I held the phone away from my ear. "PIPPI!"

"You aren't going to believe what happened last night," I said. "You know I like to be the center of attention, but this was over the top." I told her about the cat fight and getting swarmed afterward.

"You're killing me, Pips," she said. "No fair you having so much fun without me."

"Truth be told, I was a little freaked," I said. "I didn't know what would happen ... if I'd end up hurt or in jail or what."

"You asked to be a lady wrestler, lady," she said. "Lady wrestlers stage fake fights and roll around on bar floors, apparently."

"That's not the only thing that happened," I said. "Giselle was hitting on Billie, and they made out in the back seat of my car the whole way home."

"Wrestlers in love," Connie said. "So romantic."

"Speaking of love, how about you?" I asked. "How're things going with the locksmith?"

"Great," she said. " Very steady. She says what she's going to do and does it. Sexiest thing in the world."

"You deserve it," I said. "Take it slow, okay? But give it time to see if she's a psycho before you fall in love. Speaking of which, I met someone last night."

"Romantic or a friend?" she asked.

"Not sure," I said. "He's kind of nerdy, kind of cute. I said I'd go to a movie with him. I'll let you know how it goes."

She filled me in on the paper (nobody fired or hired last week) and we promised to talk soon. I felt so much better. I got ready for bed and fell asleep quickly.

I was dreaming of the world's best Cuban sandwich from the Silver Ring in Ybor City when I jolted awake to the sound of gunshots. Dogs barking. Someone yelling. Then, a bellowing like a wounded elephant. I checked the clock: 2 a.m. I peeked through the blinds.

Next door a bare-chested man swayed on widespread feet. Wolfgang wore nothing but white boxers and his tall black boots. He used his rifle as a cane, the only way he was standing upright. Something caught his attention and he stumbled toward the house. Leaning against the handrail for balance, he shifted the rifle to his shoulder and fired again into the night sky.

I had to get away. The flimsy walls of my home wouldn't stop a bullet. I tiptoed to the kitchen with my running shoes. I opened the back window slowly and pushed out the screen. I eased myself down slowly but dead leaves crackled when I hit the ground. I was sure he'd hear. I froze and held my breath. Another shot split the darkness. Wolfgang screamed about Crystal dancing "too damn close to that cowboy." From inside the house, she yelled back that he was "out of his god-damn mind."

I leaned around the edge of my house. While his back was turned I sprinted to a large pine tree by the lake. He fired another shot into the air. I took the back path to Giselle's and tapped on her door. No one answered, so I let myself in. I felt my way in the dark to the couch. My legs shaking so hard they barely held me up. Giselle, and then Billie, emerged from the bedroom.

"What's going on?" Giselle said, rubbing sleep from her eyes. They sat down on either side of me.

"Can't you hear that? The guy next door is out of his mind," I said. "He and Crystal are screaming at each other and he's got a gun. We've got to call the police." I jumped up, ready to head to Moolah's for the phone, but they each grabbed an arm and pulled me down.

"We're not calling the police," Billie said. "That's what Wolfgang does. Every couple of months, he gets trashed and shoots his gun. Crystal'll be fine."

Their sleep-warmed bodies made me feel less afraid. Once my shakes subsided, Giselle brought me a pillow and a blanket. They headed back to bed. I spent a long time listening for gunshots, but the storm had passed. Eventually, I drifted into dreams of monsters chasing me through fields of sucking mud.

Chapter 17

MONKEY FLIP

W ake up!" Giselle yanked the blankets off me. "Work-out in 30 minutes!"

I felt like I'd just closed my eyes. "Noooooo," I moaned. I turned over to go back to sleep, but Giselle poked me hard. I barely had time to slip on my shoes before she was shoving me out the door with a steaming cup of instant coffee.

Across the lake, everything looked remarkably calm, beautiful even. I walked home, stopping to sip my coffee. The nearer I got to my place, the faster my heart beat. Nothing was stirring and there was no evidence of the previous night's mayhem except for some scuffed dirt in the front of their house.

I splashed water on my face, pulled on running shorts and a tank top, and ate a banana before sprinting to the ring. Everyone was there. Linda was talking, her back to me. Brandy and Giselle were whispering. I rolled into the ring and crouched behind Wanda. Linda announced that we'd be learning the monkey flip.

"This is a flashy way to get your opponent on her back," she said, gesturing for Giselle to stand in front of her.

"I put my hands behind her neck," Linda said. "Then I jump up on her thighs and fall backward. I pull her with me as I fall back and then push her off with my legs. If you push hard enough, you can fly her to the opposite side of the ring where she lands on her back."

I was anxious and aching. Holy crap, I thought. Not this. Not today.

"You ready?" she asked. Giselle nodded. Linda hopped on Giselle's thighs for a second before falling back and flipping Giselle across the ring. Despite my exhaustion, the move looked like it might be fun.

"Line up," Linda barked.

Giselle walked to where I was standing. I raised an eyebrow.

"Piece of cake," she whispered.

"Even for me?"

She nodded. "No problem."

One by one, Linda monkey flipped us to show us how it was supposed to feel. Next, we flipped each other. At the height of the flip, I felt like I was flying.

Giselle walked out with me afterward. "You okay?" she asked. "Guess you didn't get much sleep last night."

"Thanks for letting me crash with you," I said, adding. "You and Billie?" She shushed me.

"Aren't you worried about Moolah?" I asked when we'd moved away from the others.

"I don't think she'd boot Billie. She can make money off of her," Giselle said. "But we're keeping it quiet. Please don't say anything to anyone, not even to Brandy. She's got a big mouth."

"Tell me something I don't know," I said. "I'd die if you got kicked out." She smiled and gave me a quick hug. After practice, we went our separate ways. There was still no sign of life next door. Wolfgang and his girlfriend were probably sleeping it off.

I was starving and sweating, so I showered and fixed a PB and J, heavy on the peanut butter. I was mid-bite when the phone rang.

"Hello?" I said, moving the food to my cheek, chipmunk style.

"Hi Pippi," a voice said. "It's Keith. We met at Group Therapy the other night?"

"Oh, hi Keith." I had to spit out my bite to respond, my stomach growling. My sandwich seemed way more tempting than this phone call.

"I'm calling to see if you'd like to catch that movie," he said. "Any night's good, even tonight."

No way was I going out tonight. I needed time to recuperate. I suggested the following Sunday. I could tell he was disappointed, but his emotions weren't my problem. We hung up and I finished lunch.

The afternoon practice was a full-on disaster. Linda started us on the ropes. She showed us how to run flat out, turning at the last minute and throwing ourselves sideways against the ropes. The slight elasticity of the ropes would supposedly cause us to spring back to the other side of the ring.

"Okay, one at a time," Linda yelled.

Brandy was first. She was so short, the first time she tried to hit the ropes, she went through the gap between the top and middle rope. She hit the apron with a loud thud and slipped to the floor. Everyone crowded around. A hand appeared on the apron, then her eyes. She pulled herself up. A thin trickle of blood dribbled down her chin. Linda handed her a mashed tissue.

"Again," Linda said. "A fat lip ain't going to kill you. What will kill you is not knowing how to do this."

"I can't," Brandy wailed, rolling back into the ring.

Giselle clapped her on the back. "Give it a try," she said. "You can do it."

Brandy took a deep breath and ran toward the ropes. This time, she held her arm high so there was no chance she'd slip through the gap. She leaned into the ropes and sprang a foot and a half in the air toward the other side of the ring.

I had the opposite problem as Brandy. I had to remain in a crouch to get down to the level of the top rope. I ran and hit the ropes hard, pain searing my ribs. On my second try, I ran a little slower and hit the ropes. It still hurt like hell.

At home, I peeled off the damp tank top and looked in the mirror. Dark red welts, each an inch wide, striped my right side from my armpit to my hip.

Linda was on fire all week. She ran us through new move after new move—body slam (fun), clothesline (easy), and face-on-the-rope-rake (obviously fake). Time flew. Between learning moves and extra hours at Kinko's, I hit the mattress and was asleep within minutes every night.

By Sunday, all I wanted to do was stay home and read a book, maybe make chili. But I heaved myself out of bed and into the shower. Keith was waiting.

Chapter 18

FIRST DATE

K eith was sitting on the porch of a tidy white house when I drove up. I parked in his driveway, butterflies in my stomach. I wasn't sure if I was interested in "that way" so I hadn't dressed up. Still, I looked pretty cute in my shorts and t-shirt.

The wicker chair squeaked when he got up to greet me. He reached out to shake my hand just as I went in for a kiss on his cheek. Out of the tangle, he got a handful of my right breast. I blushed and he yanked his hand back as if burned.

"Any trouble finding the place?"

"No, your directions were perfect," I said.

He held open the screen door for me, which led directly into the kitchen. Spotless counters and new appliances provided a sharp contrast to my grody hearth. He was very neat and I wondered if he was my type.

"The movie's in an hour, but if we miss that show, there's another one later," he said, with kind eyes. "So, no rush."

To the left of the kitchen, an eggplant-colored sectional sofa dominated the large living room. Color is practically my religion, so my eyelids fluttered when I caught sight of the teal blue throw pillows. Across the room, French doors opened into an office filled with three large dining room tables. Cardboard boxes filled every inch of table space. A large model of the Starship Enterprise hovered in the airspace above the boxes. Clearly, this was geek HQ.

Stacks of cardboard boxes also lined the shelves. Plastic-clad comic books labeled by name, date, and issue number filled each box. He was organized, a quality I envied and hoped to cultivate at some point in my life.

"I have something to show you," he said, reaching for a box marked X-men. He pulled out a comic and carefully removed it from its plastic sheath. He hesitated.

"Do you mind washing your hands before handling it?" he asked.

I winced inwardly but didn't kick up a fuss. The bathroom was a treat, festooned as it was in 1950s science fiction movie posters, including "Attack of the 50 FT. Woman."

By the time I'd returned, he had moved to the giant couch and patted the cushion next to him. He'd set wine glasses on coasters on the far side of the coffee table. I sat next to him, a foot of space between us.

"This is what I wanted to show you," he said. On the cover was the image of a muscular Black woman in biker gear, and best of all, sporting a mohawk.

"Cool! Who's that?"

"Her name is Storm. She's a very kick-ass, take-no-prisoners kind of gal, kind of like you," he said, giving me a look and holding my gaze. My stomach did a little flip but I couldn't decide if it was attraction or embarrassment. I riffled through the pages of the comic.

"So what's her story?"

Storm, he explained, was the daughter of a Kenyan witch-priestess and a photojournalist. The couple had settled in Harlem, where Storm was born, and then moved to Egypt.

A bomb demolished their apartment, killing the parents and leaving six-year-old Storm buried under tons of rubble.

"She's a skilled weather witch and thief," he said. "And claustrophobic."

I examined her more closely. The illustrator hadn't tried to turn her into a Barbie doll. She had muscles and looked tough enough. I especially loved the mohawk, the ultimate bad-ass haircut. I was looking for a wrestling persona to distinguish myself and Storm's look felt right. I wondered what Giselle and Billie would think.

"You mind if I borrow this?" I asked, holding up the comic.

"Sure. Just promise you'll take care of it," Keith said, smiling. He returned the comic to its plastic sheath. He sealed it and passed it over. Another check in the "pro-Keith" column.

We drifted to the porch to enjoy the breeze. While we asked and answered all the getting-to-know-you questions, a middle-aged man in scruffy work clothes wandered up. He held his head down as if tacking into a big wind. He clearly had been drinking.

"Gotta cigarette?" he slurred, raising his head slightly. The lower lids of his eyes rested like red bowls on his cheeks. A few seconds later, his odor hit me in the face: booze, cigarettes, body odor, with a soupçon of piss.

"Nope, sorry," I said, standing and moving away.

Keith hadn't moved. "Can I make you a sandwich?" he offered.

The shabby man looked at Keith and nodded slowly. Keith had one foot over the threshold when the man added, "And some of that wine you're drinking." I frowned.

"What's up?" I asked. "On a bender?"

Determining that an answer would be some kind of payment for the sandwich, he said, "I finished working a big construction job a couple of days ago and went out for drinks with my buddies. I kept going until this morning. I must've gotten rolled last night cause my rent money is gone." He pulled out his empty pockets.

He looked toward the door, both of us willing Keith to come out with the damn sandwich. The sound of a knife falling on a plate told us that it was still in the works.

"Almost there," Keith called out.

"My wife's going to be so pissed," he said, rubbing his face. "Rent's due and my baby needs milk."

"How old's your baby?" I asked.

"Just turned four," he said, looking down at his feet. "I should've gone straight home. I'm such a fuck-up."

Keith was standing in the doorway, holding a plate and a large plastic cup. I reached him in three steps.

"Yes, to the sandwich. No, to the wine." I passed the man the sandwich and grabbed the big plastic cup filled with at least a third of a bottle of wine. The man's pleading eyes followed me back inside. I brought him a coke instead.

The man balanced the paper plate on the banister and tore into the sandwich. It was gone in four bites and he downed the soda just as quickly.

"Why don't we give this guy a lift home," I suggested. "Maybe stop off at a grocery first."

"Good idea," he said. "But we don't need to go to the store. I have tons of food here. I'll pack a couple of bags. We can still catch the flick."

"Do you have milk?" I asked. "He said his little girl needs milk."

"I have an unopened gallon he can have," Keith said and went back inside.

"I don't know if this is such a good idea," the man started.

"I bet they'll be glad to know you're okay. And they'll have something to eat." We piled into Keith's sports car, windows all the way down.

Twenty minutes later, we pulled into a working-class neighborhood. He directed Keith to a small house surrounded by a chain-link fence. A pit bull barked at us from a yard two houses down. His house was one of the few with a tree. Dangling from one of the sturdier branches, a tiny girl sat in a tire swing. A thin woman in a lime-green house dress stood behind her, giving her little pushes.

"Daddy!" she cried, her face bright as a blossom. She slid out of the swing and skipped over to the car. She grabbed his legs and buried her face between his knees, despite his stink. He reached down to touch her head, but his expression was stony. His wife stood frozen for a few seconds next to the swing. She reached out and stilled the swing and walked to him on leaden feet.

"I'm Pippi and this is Keith," I called, walking toward the front door. "Okay to bring the groceries inside?"

She nodded, barely turning her head. The little girl brought her mother into the embrace, holding their legs in her tiny arms. At the threshold, I looked back. The adults were staring at each other, linked by their daughter.

Blankets covered the living room window to keep the heat out. The fridge was bare except for a jar of mustard and half a sleeve of saltines.

"We got here in the nick of time." I looked over at Keith. "Thanks for doing this." I reached over and kissed his cheek.

The little girl led her parents to the house and we got out of there. Good deed done, we drove to the movies and got in line for tickets. He pulled out a crisp twenty.

"So, are you a trust fund baby?" I asked him as we neared the head of the line.

He frowned, "Why'd you ask that?"

"Nice house, amazing kitchen, and lots of collectibles. I haven't heard you talk about work. It's either that or drug dealer," I joked.

"My parents bought me the house to live in while I was in college. I graduated a few years ago," he said. "They set aside money so I didn't have to worry about finding a job right away. But I'm not rich."

"Do your parents live in Columbia?" I asked.

"They're over in Waterloo," he said. "It's a little town not far from here."

"You didn't live at home while you were in college?"

"Nah, the house where I grew up is a pit," he said. "It's a nice house, probably the biggest in the town, but it hasn't been cleaned in 20 years. Not since my mom found out that my dad was having an affair."

"They couldn't get a housekeeper?" I asked.

"He was stubborn. Said he brought home the bacon and she sat home all day. He wasn't going to pay someone to do her job."

"Sounds rough," I said.

"I was really young when it started so it's all I ever knew," he said. "None of my friends ever came over."

I flashed on a child standing on a chair in front of the stove while his parents waited for dinner at either end of a long table. It made me sad so I changed the subject.

"Tell me about the movie we're going to see," I asked.

Keith got carried away talking about the dusty world of "Dune." He painted pictures of a water-starved planet and giant worms that produced spice necessary for space travel. He recited a passage from the book.

"I must not fear. Fear is the mind-killer. Fear is the little-death that brings total obliteration. I will face my fear. I will permit it to pass over me and through me." A faraway siren punctuated the end of the recitation.

A knot of tension, which I hadn't even been aware of loosened. Worry about the shotgun incident, the sad man we'd encountered, and memories of my own flawed father fell away.

It was after 10 when we got back to his house. The wine had worn off and it was time to head home. He told me to wait and came back holding the X-men comic with the Storm character.

"Take care," he said, giving me a quick hug. "I hope we can do it again real soon."

Chapter 19

FLYING HEAD SCISSORS

Mohawked women flashed through my dream forests. Warrior women mushed huskies in northernmost Norway, while others beat off villains in "Blade Runner" cityscapes. Before waking, I found myself floating in a sapphire mountain lake, my rainbow mohawk jutting skyward. Just before waking, I swam toward a buff man waiting on the shore. Electricity shot through me, a lingering tingle to go with my espresso.

After showering and dressing, I had 15 minutes to examine Storm, the comic book character. Her long white mohawk curved around her high cheekbones. Black leather gauntlets were strapped to her wrists. A skintight biker top showed off muscular arms. A wide choker graced her long neck. I was excited at developing my wrestling persona based on elements of Storm's costume. At two minutes to practice, I sprinted across the lake road and slid into the circle surrounding Linda.

"You won't use this move all the time, but when you do, the crowds will go wild," she said. "I'll talk you through it."

In the flying head scissors, she told us to run fast toward our opponent and throw ourselves sideways into the air. "Your legs need to be near your opponent's neck so she can thread her head between your ankles," Linda explained. "Once she has a hold of you, she'll wait a beat while you straighten yourself across her shoulders. You should look like the top part of a 'T,' " she said, making the time-out hand signal. "Your opponent takes a bump onto her back with your legs still wrapped around her neck, so it looks like you're flipping her with the strength of your legs."

Linda narrowed her eyes at me. "Stretch, you work with Zoey since she's the closest to your height." Zoey looked at Linda like she was crazy but didn't say anything. I hated going first but there was no room to protest.

"Okay if I try to catch you first?" I asked Zoey. "It looks a little easier than scissoring you around the neck." Zoey grumbled but agreed.

I stood several feet in front of the turnbuckle and positioned my right foot a little ahead of my left for stability, just as Linda had shown us. I nodded that I was ready and Zoey charged. I had underestimated the impact of 160 pounds of flying woman. She threw her legs in the air and though I tried to thread my head through her ankles, the force of the impact was too much. We both went down hard. Zoey was not happy.

"Again," Linda barked.

Zoey had a whispered conversation with Linda, who shook her head and pushed her to the middle of the ring. This time, when Zoey flew at me, I knew to push into it and rebalance.

"Okay, now straighten up, Stretch," Linda instructed. "Zoey's going to redistribute her weight. Wait two beats and then take a bump. And don't break your neck."

I stepped off my right foot like I would in a normal bump. I landed on my back with Zoey still attached. She pushed herself up on her arms and gave my neck a hard squeeze. It was clear that this was payback. I wedged my fingers under her calves, but she squeezed even harder. I pinched the back of her knee and she finally eased up. She really didn't like me.

"That's enough," Linda said. "Your turn, Stretch."

I looked over at Giselle, cold dread pooling in my stomach. She smiled and gave me a thumb's up. There was nothing to do but take my position in the corner opposite Zoey. She looked worried and who could blame her? I outweighed her by 10 pounds and I'd never done a move this complicated.

I sprinted toward her and pitched myself into the air. As if in slow motion, I saw that my feet were (miraculously) near her head where they were supposed to be but my legs were uneven. I tried to correct my position midair and ended up kicking Zoey in the teeth. We both dropped to the mat. I landed on my stomach unhurt, but blood smeared Zoey's mouth.

"I'm so sorry." I tried to smooth back the hair from her face, but she smacked my hand. She got up and stalked toward Linda, holding her mouth. Drops of blood stained her shirt.

"Told you," she said and scooted out of the ring. She was done working with me. I headed to the back of the line, completely mortified.

Giselle stepped up and volunteered, "I'll catch her."

Linda and I both stared at her. I was half a foot taller and 50 pounds heavier and Giselle thought she could catch me?

"I'm shorter than Zoey, so she won't have to jump so high," she reasoned.

Linda nodded and we took our respective corners. After a couple of deep breaths, I pelted toward her, threw my legs in the air and, miracle of miracles, she ducked her head and caught me around her neck.

She took one small step back to regain her balance. I locked my ankles and then straightened my body across her shoulders, pushing against her hip to distribute my weight. Then she stepped into a perfect bump. We ended up with me on my side and my ankles around her neck. We lay there a second, not quite believing it.

The other trainees whooped. Wanda reached down and offered me a hand up while Brandy clapped Giselle on the back. A hummingbird of a smile flitted across Linda's face and then she told everyone to shut up and get back to work.

We traded places. Giselle charged toward me, threw herself in the air and I caught her easily. I gave her a second to straighten up and then took the bump. Once I'd gotten over the fear of breaking my neck, the move was balletic.

Back in line, we high-fived. "Be careful of Zoey. She's going to potato you first chance she gets," Giselle whispered. "I know her. She'll try to get you back."

After practice, I jogged home to shower and grab Keith's comic before going over to Giselle's. I was hoping for a few minutes alone with her before Billie or Brandy showed up. Even though I felt silly, I asked her to wash her hands before opening the comic.

"Sorry, the guy who owns it is a little anal." We sat side by side at her kitchen table.

"What do you think about this character?" I said, pointing at Storm. "As something I could use for my gimmick."

"You'd really get a mohawk?" she looked at me with wide eyes. "That would be amazing. Double dog dare you!"

"Double dog dare me? Well, I guess I'll have to do it now," I joked, pointing out parts of the character's costume that I liked best.

"I want to hit the Harley store outside town for some biker boots and some spiked gauntlets," I said. "How about you? Have you decided what your look will be?" She ran her fingers through her blond mop.

"Moolah wants me to be a but I really, really, really want to be a heel. It's a family tradition." We talked some more about how she could develop a heel look.

"The costume isn't as important as the vibe you put off," she said, demonstrating a full-on scowl and growl. She furrowed her brow and turned down the corners of her mouth. If I hadn't known what a sweetheart she was, I might've been more convinced.

I wanted to try it, so we went into the bathroom and practiced our heel faces. After a while, we burst out laughing.

"I can't wait until they start teaching us how to put the moves together," I said. "Tell me again what they call it when you act like something really hurts?"

"That's called 'selling.' That's what the older girls practice in the evening," she said, admitting that she sometimes snuck in to watch them.

"I already know the score, about it being a work. You know, 'fake'," Giselle said. "And Moolah owes me for sending me to Howie way back when. Anyway, they let me stay."

"When do they practice?" I said. "I want to come see!"

"You've got to be careful," she said. "Wait until after dark, when the lights in the practice ring come on. Do not get caught. Darlene's tough."

She noticed me poking at the six-inch bruises on my elbows. I kept feeling for little bits of bone that had chipped off my elbow and now floated in the swollen jelly. I obsessively checked to make sure they hadn't migrated to other parts of my body.

"You ever think about elbow pads?" Giselle asked.

"Yeah, but I thought you were considered a wuss if you wore them," I said, immediately regretting my remark. Giselle always wore kneepads to help with her trick knee.

"Screw that," she said. "It's your body. You've got to protect yourself."

∞

That evening, I was getting ready for my second date with Keith. I noticed that the lights in the training ring were on. I didn't think twice. Hairbrush in hand, I jogged toward the workout ring.

The dogs started barking the closer I got to the building. I could hear noise behind the door, which was cracked open. I peeked through in time to see Moolah snatch someone by the hair and shove her into a rough chokehold. The old faces soaked up the maestro's lesson. I pushed open the door a couple of inches more and saw that Zoey was Moolah's opponent.

"Don't be gentle. She can take it," Moolah growled.

Zoey grabbed Moolah's wrists to control the tug on her hair but it still looked excruciating. So that was selling, I thought as I felt a sharp kick on my shins. I looked down into the accusing face of Darlene, Moolah's diminutive enforcer.

"You ain't supposed to be here," she said. Though she was only 3'6", she shoved me out of the doorway. I stepped back.

"I don't want to see you or any of the other new faces down here again, got it?" she said. "Moolah will let you know when you can train with the real wrestlers. Now, fuck off."

She went back inside and slammed the door. I could hear the cackles of the old faces and my face burned.

"You've got to be kidding me," I fumed to myself. "I'm killing myself training four hours a day and she won't even teach me how to sell?" Then I remembered that I was supposed to head downtown.

Keith was reading a comic on the front porch when I drove up.

"It looks like you need a hug," he said, reaching for me. I did, in fact, need a hug but I wished it wasn't so obvious. I definitely needed to work on my poker face. He wrapped his long arms around me and squeezed gently at first.

"Harder," I said. "Hug me harder." I melted into him, letting go of all the tension. My back cracked and he stood back alarmed.

"Did I hurt you?" he asked.

"No, it felt good," I said, reaching out for him again. When he released me a second time, I took a deep breath, equilibrium restored.

"There's nothing like a good bear hug," I said. "That hug's the only physical contact I've had in weeks that didn't come with a pain chaser."

"Any more wine left?" I nodded to his glass on the side table. Pretty soon we were both relaxing on the front porch talking over our days.

"The thing I don't understand is why they don't teach us the stuff they actually do in the ring. What's the point of keeping it a secret?"

"If I had to guess, I'd say Moolah wants to keep you in training for as long as possible to keep you paying rent," Keith said. "It's a pretty good racket."

I asked him about his day. "Not bad, actually," he said. "Did I mention that I'm writing a short story about Nikola Tesla?" He told me all about how Tesla thought he had heard radio signals from Mars and tried to beam messages back.

"I thought it'd be cool to write a story where Tesla actually makes contact with Martians."

Keith refilled my glass. He explained that Tesla had invented the light bulb rather than Edison. He said that Tesla also invented radar, hydroelectric energy, transistors, neon lighting, and remote control. Tesla spoke eight languages, Keith explained, and never had sex because it would interfere with his work.

"Sounds like a cool dude. All except for the celibacy," I said, joking.

Instead of laughing, he gave me an intense look that sent energy surging through me. He reached out and brought my hand to his lips. He stood, tugging me toward him until we stood belly to belly. I could feel his pulse jackhammering like mine. I watched his full sensual lips as he slowly moved in for a kiss. As a connoisseur of kisses, I was pleasantly surprised that he was the rarest of male creatures, a man who saw kissing as a destination itself.

I'd been without sex for almost two months and was as voracious as a tiger eyeing a toothsome water buffalo. I didn't want to scare him so I allowed him to dance me from the porch to the front door, never breaking the kiss. We stumbled over the threshold and he kicked the door closed behind us. The couch was closer than the bed so we fell upon it and each other.

We broke apart long enough to rip off each other's shirts. He pulled me on top of him and reached around with both hands to undo my bra. We kissed and nibbled each other until I couldn't stand it anymore. I reached for his belt and the bulge behind the zipper. I wasn't prepared for his blue superman underwear and burst out laughing. I reassured him that I found them adorable but was more interested to see what was underneath. My whole body was flushed, infused with desire. My pulse skipped wildly as I slipped out of my shorts.

"Do you have rubbers?" I asked with a sinking feeling. He ran to his bedside table in the next room. He groaned when I slipped on the Trojan XL and climbed aboard, sliding slowly up and down, careful not to go too deep. A few strokes and I came. With the worst of my hunger slaked, I was able to go more slowly, building up to a rafter-shaking, howl-at-the-moon double orgasm. He stared at me like I was magic. I stopped at three and let him take a turn. He rolled over on top of me, pumped a few times, and came trembling and moaning. We nestled together for a nap, woke up and fucked again. I was sore but blissful when I left his place early the next morning.

Chapter 20

THE BLACK NEWS

I relaxed during the morning practice, floating on memories of the previous night. Giselle raised an eyebrow at me and made the universal sign of an index finger inserted into a circled finger and thumb. I smiled and nodded. I don't even remember what we learned that morning. Pleasurable tremors ran through my body.

Somehow, I made it through practice and, after a quick shower, headed to my 11 a.m. shift at the copy shop. Dave was filling orders but the line was still out the door. I stepped in to assist a wispy-bearded graduate student, impatient for copies of his dissertation on hydrocarbons in Morocco. Bleh, boring. I handed him boxes of his bound work and he slouched out of the store. We whittled down the line until all the customers had been helped.

Before the next rush, we restocked paper. Mid-way through the task, the doorbell chimed, as a couple of well-dressed African-American men entered. We waited while they finished their conversation.

"It's the first time they've shown their faces in Columbia in more than a decade," said the taller man in a grey pinstripe suit. "I thought we had made it clear the last time that our town wasn't in the market for their nonsense. But it's a major news story that affects our community and the Black News has got to cover it." I perked up at the name of the newspaper.

The other man, in a navy blazer, shook his head. "You saw what happened in Greensboro. I'm not saying our police force would drop the ball like theirs did, but it wouldn't take much for people to start pulling out guns and playing cowboy. I don't care how many cops they have at the rally, it's not safe to send a reporter." They were keeping their voices low but I couldn't help but overhear them.

"In a democratic society, the newspaper has to be a watchdog over activities that might harm our citizens," the taller one said. "You think The State will cover it? I have no confidence they will or, if they did, that their coverage will speak to the concerns of our readers."

"I can't stand when you get on your high horse, but I have to agree with you. We have to cover it. But we can't send one of our reporters into the lion's den. That leaves us with a problem and not much time to solve it," navy blazer said.

The taller man put his briefcase on the counter and pulled out a single page. It spelled out plans for a peaceful demonstration in response to a Ku Klux Klan rally being held in Columbia two weeks from Saturday. A paramilitary branch of the KKK from North Carolina was holding the rally to recruit new members, according to the flyer. He asked for 500 copies on yellow paper.

It was like I'd stepped into some hideous time machine jettisoning me to an era when racists still ran around in white sheets and hoods. Dave took the page and went to make the copies.

"I couldn't help but overhearing your conversation," I said. "I may have a solution to your problem. My name's Pippi. If

you're looking for a reporter to cover the Klan rally, I can do it."
I stood up straight and tugged the hem of my Devo T-shirt.

Now it was their turn to boggle. They both pulled their
heads back and stared. The copy shop girl wanted to cover a
Klan rally for them?

"I graduated a couple of years ago with a journalism degree
from the University of South Florida," I said. "I worked for
almost two years at a newspaper near Tampa. I have clips and
references. And I'm a pretty good photographer if you want
pictures."

I could see them sizing me up, wondering if big blond Aryan
me was too good to be true. They introduced themselves:
the taller man was Tyrell Beauchamp and the older man was
Charles Jefferson. Together, they published the Black News.

"Pardon me if this seems rude, but if you have a journalism
degree, why in the world are you working at Kinko's?" Tyrell
said. He had a point.

"I'll be happy to tell you but that's a conversation I'd prefer
to have in private," I said, glancing back at Dave who was
finishing up their job.

I hadn't told Dave about the wrestling camp though he'd
often asked about my bruises. I just told him I was accident-
prone. I wanted to let him in on my secret, but in the back of
my mind, I could hear my mom telling me that small towns
have big ears. I think he knew there was more to my story, but
he didn't press me.

"Why don't you swing by the office after you get off work,"
said Tyrell. He jotted down directions to the newspaper, a mile
away on Harden Street. Their offices were housed in a yellow
brick building.

"God works in mysterious ways," Charles said, shaking my
hand. "I'm glad our copier chose today to break down."

Dave was cool about letting me leave early. When I arrived, a pretty receptionist stood and walked me through to the inner sanctum where Tyrell and Charles sat at a round table with two other men, all in shirtsleeves. The air conditioner in the small office chugged bravely but it put out barely kept pace with the scorching temperature. Sweat ringed the armpits of their starched white shirts. Each man kept a handkerchief and a fan close at hand.

Tyrell gestured to a chair and introduced me to the other men, who worked on the advertising and production sides of the paper.

I talked about reporting for the Sun newspaper. "I interviewed some fascinating people but eventually I got bored." I told them about wanting to learn how to wrestle as part of a journalism project. I bit the inside of my cheek. I had barely written anything beyond a few journal entries getting to my first bump. I pushed the thought away.

"I'm interested in challenging journalism projects and covering a Klan rally for the Black News fits the bill," I said.

Charles nodded. "You should go into this with your eyes wide open. There is some risk of bodily harm. Of course, we'll pay you."

He explained that it had only been five years since a local communist workers party had planned a "Death to the Klan" march in Greensboro, N.C. Protestors were supposed to gather at noon at a housing project but before the march got started, members of the Klan and the American Nazi Party had killed five protesters and wounded 11 others.

"No one ever went to prison," he said. "This is the same group that's holding the rally in our town." I was surprised that I had missed this story when it happened.

"Where were the police?" I asked.

"Most of them were having lunch," he said. "The march permit was for noon, so their commanders told them to show up on location at 11:30. They decided to have lunch beforehand and that's when the melee broke out."

"Our situation's a little different," Charles said. "When they announced the rally, the Klan made a big ballyhoo saying thousands of people would show up. Our chief of police took that seriously and said that a downtown rally was out of the question. A few days ago, they approved a permit for a rally at a farm 20 miles outside of town. That'll cut down on attendance. We are not going to have a repeat of the 1979 Greensboro Massacre."

"I understand what you're saying. It's dangerous," I said, looking each of them in the eye. "I want to do it. The question is, do you want me?" I offered to leave the room so they could talk it over in private. Tyrell shook his head.

"If you're willing and believe you can do it, then you're hired." We spent the rest of the hour hashing out the details. I had to leave for practice but promised to be in touch for further instructions.

I barely made it to the afternoon practice on time. I had to share the good news with somebody, so I called Connie that evening. She wasn't exactly thrilled.

"I don't like the sound of this," she said. "Who knows what they might do when they're wearing those ridiculous costumes. I grew up around these backward assholes, Pippi. They can be dangerous, especially in a group. You have to be careful."

"I'll be fine," I said, not sure if I believed it. But I wasn't going to be dissuaded from my first freelance gig.

Taking the job meant missing a Saturday practice, which would take some finessing. I'd seen Linda order Brandy to take 20 fast bumps for showing up 20 minutes late.

I approached Linda before first practice the next day. To soften her up, I handed her a good cup of Cuban coffee. She raised an eyebrow.

"I need a favor," I said. "Kinko's has a big order and they asked me to do a double-shift on the Saturday after next. I'd have to miss the afternoon practice."

She glowered at me, daring me to continue.

"I'd like to make up for it by cleaning the mat and sweeping out the training room," I looked at her, but she wasn't biting. "For two weeks," I added.

Wiping down the matt with a bleachy mop was a job that new faces got stuck with. After a while, bodily fluids crusted up on the mat and could make the wrestlers sick. She inhaled the coffee aroma and took a sip.

"Just this once," she said. "You'll clean the ring, sweep the floor, and bring me a cup of this coffee before morning practice for two weeks."

We struck the deal and I wordlessly thanked my Cuban-American friends in Tampa for teaching me the right way to make cafe con leche.

After practice, I stopped by Giselle's place. I said "hi" to Billie, who had already found her spot on the couch. I barely got through the front door when Giselle asked, "So, how's your love life?"

"Pretty good," I admitted. "Keith's a sweetie."

"Are you in looooove?" she asked, pulling out the word like saltwater taffy.

"He's not Mr. Right. But he's pretty good for Mr. Right Now."

"You can't tell when you're going to fall in love," Giselle said, shooting Billie a steamy look.

"Yes I can," I said. "I'm not giving my heart away. I've got too many places I want to go to get tied down. You're the ones who have to be careful."

"Look, you can't say anything about us being together because Moolah'd kick us out," Giselle said.

"Duh. Y'all do whatever you please. I won't say a thing." I asked.

"Moolah's a hypocrite because I know for a fact she runs both ways," Billie said.

I raised my eyebrows.

"What do you mean?"

"We were on the road together," Billie said. "After the matches one night, she shows up at my hotel room a little drunk. Told me she just wanted a kiss before bedtime. I told her I wasn't interested. She went back to her room, but that vindictive bitch got back at me. The next couple of months I had almost no bookings."

Pimp, sexual harasser, thief. How low could this woman sink?

"Well, that's just fucking hypocritical," I said.

"Yeah, but she's the boss and can do what she likes," Giselle said, shrugging.

Chapter 21

KEISTER BOUNCE

The next morning, I hot-footed to Linda's door with her coffee. Not being a morning person, she accepted the tribute with slit eyes and a grunt. She took the coffee and closed the door on me without a word. Fifteen minutes later, she slid into the ring and got straight to work.

"Today, we are going to work on something called the keister bounce," she said.

In this move, Linda explained, you sit behind your opponent with your legs wrapped around her waist and your hands hooked under her armpits.

"You rock backward and you push her as high in the air as you can and slam her down on her keister," she said.

It sounded goofy but I wasn't going to say anything. Linda paired me up with Wanda, much to my chagrin. She was a heavy woman and would be hard to push skyward. But it wasn't so bad. All it really took was a rocking motion and then a really strong upward thrust.

"Does it hurt when you hit?" I asked her after the first bounce.

"Not a bit," she said. "It's fun."

I bounced her a few times and then we traded places and

she did the same to me. Giselle and Brandy paired up to do the move and that's when I understood the point of the exercise. Anyone sitting in front of the two wrestlers—the ones who paid premium prices for their seats—got a two-for-one crotch shot.

As fun as the move was, it was also kind of humiliating. I was pretty sure you wouldn't catch men wrestlers doing it. When it came time for real matches, I wouldn't be doing it either.

We practiced the bounce for a while and then moved on to the step-over toehold. Linda instructed Giselle, her guinea pig, to lie down on the mat, then picked up her left leg and stepped over it. She locked Giselle's foot under her upper arm.

"You can twist your opponent's foot to put more pressure on it," Linda said. "You can also push down the leg to apply pressure to the hip and knee." We practiced the nothing move, which was even easier than a keister bounce.

Brandy whispered. "What are you all doing tonight? Should I come over?"

"I can't. I've got stuff to do," Giselle said. Not that she'd ask me but I couldn't hang out either.

I had an evening shift at Kinko's. It turned out to be a slow evening, so Dave could've handled it himself. We kept ourselves entertained by taking each other's pictures with the passport photo machine.

He had one of those skinny Jesus bodies I liked, but I was glad I'd resisted the urge to sleep with him. I had needed his friendship more than I needed anything else. Right from the beginning, with an invitation to the fish fry, he'd introduced me to cool people. He finished with a customer and came back to where I perched on a stool.

"You want to go to a potluck this weekend?" he asked. "A friend of mine is a brewer and he has these big dinners once a week. It's really fun and there's always good home-brewed beer."

"I wish I could but things are pretty busy right now," I said. The Klan rally flashed through my brain. "Raincheck?"

I headed home around 9. I'd had to park several blocks away because the theater next door was holding its annual Bogart festival. I was tempted to catch the midnight show but morning practice came so early. I was half a block from my car when I looked up.

A neon sign with the words Hair Circus twinkled from the second floor of a squarish brick building. The open sign still hung on the door, so, on a whim, I went in. Striking black and white images of pouty models lined the walls in the stairwell up to the salon. Still more images graced the waiting room. I stopped to peer at them, struck by the excellent lighting, composition and, of course, their spectacular hairdos.

"Beautiful, yes?" said a mouth underneath a mound of mahogany hair. She must be an FOP—Fan of Pippi—I thought, as I did with any redhead. Though it was midweek, she was turned out in a tailored suit in a brilliant shade of magenta. A tiny bird of a woman, she added four inches of height with black stiletto sandals. She pushed a strand of hair away from her face with an elaborately lacquered nail.

"Welcome to Hair Circus," she said. "I'm Raquel. Is there something I can help you with?"

There were no other people in the shop so I guessed she was probably closing up for the evening. But I detected a welcome rather than impatience at my arrival.

"Hi, I'm Pippi. Nice to meet you."

She smiled and looked me right in the eyes. "What can I do for you?" I trusted her immediately.

"I have kind of a weird request." I took a deep breath and

blurted out, "I'm training to be a professional wrestler and I'm looking for someone to give me a mohawk."

My request didn't throw her. On the contrary, she seemed delighted. I decided to take a chance and tell her everything. I explained how I wanted to force Moolah to start booking matches for me and that a radical haircut was part of the strategy.

"The problem is that I have fine hair and there's no way it's going to stand up like it's supposed to."

She laughed in a tinkling way that made me want to laugh. She gestured me to a salon chair and stood behind me. She ran her fingers through my hair in that instantly familiar way of hairstylists. She studied my reflection.

"I had a feeling something interesting was going to happen today. That's why I stayed late. Normally, I'd be working on my first martini by now." She pulled the top of my hair straight up. It was about seven inches long.

"Getting your hair to stand up won't be a problem, as long as you don't mind me perming the strip in the middle. Your hair needs to be roughed up to do what you want."

"How much would you charge for the cut and perm?" I asked, holding my breath. I was making ends meet working part-time at the copy shop but a big salon bill wasn't exactly in my budget.

"I'll tell you what," she said. "If you let me hang your picture—I mean a real studio portrait—in my salon, I'll give you a good deal." She put her hands on her hips and smiled. "My one condition is that you have to use my photographer."

"Thank you so much," I said. "You don't know what this means to me." We scheduled the cut for Sunday, the day after the Klan rally. That would give her plenty of time and I wouldn't have to worry about getting back to camp for practice. We shook hands and I practically skipped to my car.

When I got back to camp, I parked at Giselle's and knocked on her door. She opened the door a crack and peeked out with swollen eyes. I reined in my excitement even though I was jumping up and down on the inside.

"What's the matter?"

She wiped her nose and opened the door wide enough for me to slip in. "Nothing," she said.

"Really, Giselle, you can tell me," I said. "Maybe I can help." I could see her ready to push back but, instead, she slumped over to the couch. Used tissues had drifted to the floor where she'd been sitting.

"It's my youngest son's birthday today and I'm not there," she said. "I know they are better off where they are, but I miss them so much."

"You have kids?" I asked. "I didn't know. You want to talk about it?"

She shook her head. "That'll make it worse," she said and went into the bathroom. I could hear the water running and in a second she returned. She'd washed her face and shaken off her mood.

"Let's talk about something else," she said. "What's up with you?"

I told her about meeting Raquel and about my plan to get a mohawk like the Storm character. She gave me a big hug and immediately put me into a headlock.

"I'll go with you," she said, pretending to crank my neck. "Let's bring Billie and Brandy and make a party of it."

"Sounds good," I said, speaking to her from hip level. I let her work my neck for a while as we talked. I periodically howled in fake pain until I got tired of bending over. I grabbed the back of her thighs and threw her up in the air and fell back on the couch, a much softer cushion than the mat we trained on. The cushions fell out of the couch and we didn't bother to rearrange them. We hung out for a little while, talking about how pissed Moolah would be when she saw my new hairstyle.

Chapter 22

PREPPING FOR THE RALLY

The week before the Klan rally sped by with heavier-than-usual practices, shifts at Kinko's, and dates with Keith. On Friday, I stopped off at the Black News to iron out the final details.

"There's going to be a big police presence at the rally," Tyrell said. "South Carolina may fly the confederate flag over the state capitol, but we aren't going to let a bunch of North Carolina thugs recruit our citizens."

"Any idea how many people will show?" I asked, accepting a stack of reporter's notebooks from him.

"No way of knowing," he said. "Got your camera loaded? Take extra film and batteries," he said, pointing to a box on the round table. I scooped up several rolls of film.

"Just so you know, we decided to cancel the protest," Tyrell said. "We decided that your article and photos will raise sufficient awareness in the community."

I had a lousy afternoon practice and told Giselle I wouldn't be stopping by. I was nervous and planning on making it an early night so I'd be fresh for the rally. Around 8, I thought I'd relax with a beer or two. Then I knocked back some tequila. I was snoozing by 10 but I woke at 3 with a raging thirst and a banging head. I gulped a large glass of water and a handful of aspirin and drifted back to sleep. I actually felt rested when the alarm went off at 6. I fixed Linda's coffee and headed to the training ring.

My timing was a few seconds off for every move. I made a bunch of rookie mistakes, even scuffing my chin on a bad belly bump. Linda shot me hard looks, but my headache had come back and I ignored her. Giselle could tell I was feeling off and, without asking, reached up and massaged my neck while we stood in line for the next move. At the end of practice, I reminded Linda that I was going to have to miss the afternoon practice. She gave a slight nod, honoring the bargain we'd struck.

I headed home, my pulse scudding high in my throat. After showering off the sweat and dust of the ring, I threw on a T-shirt and jeans for my shift at Kinko's. I packed other clothes—a tight white lacey top and a short denim skirt—for the late afternoon Klan gathering. My plan was to distract them so they'd forget to ask for my news affiliation. I glanced over at Tyrell's hand-written directions to the rally. It really was in the middle of nowhere.

I performed no better at Kinko's and Dave noticed.

"What is going on with you today, Pippi?" Dave said. "It's like I'm working by myself. Are you alright?"

I couldn't keep it in. I told him about covering the Klan rally for the Black News.

"Tyrell said there'll be a lot of cops there so I shouldn't be nervous. I've interviewed lots of people before. It's not like I'm new at this." He looked at me agog.

"A Klan rally? Are you shitting me?" he said. "You should be nervous. Actually, you should be terrified. They kill people for doing stuff like you're doing. You know that, right?"

"You're not helping," I said, turning toward the back of the store. "Right now, I need you to encourage me and tell me it's going to be alright." Different responses passed across his face like clouds in a windy sky. He settled on being supportive.

"You're right. It's going to be alright," he said. "But be careful and make sure the cops know where you are at all times. Don't let them get you alone. They could do something very, very bad if they find out you're working for the Black News."

Chapter 23

KLAN RALLY

Two men in camouflage motioned me to a mostly empty field. My mind flashed back to the biker party that had set all this wrestling madness in motion. I carried nothing with the Black News logo, just my camera, extra film, notebooks, and pens. Glancing back at the parking lot, I wondered if someone would record my Florida license plate number.

I called out to one of the camo guys. "I'm looking for the head guy," I said. "I mean the Grand Dragon."

"Which one? Local or North Carolina?" he said, adjusting the brim of his rebel cap. "Well, I guess it don't matter because they're all up there," he said, pointing to a barn at the end of the dirt road.

Around the bend I froze, arrested by the sight of 40 South Carolina cops, 20 on each side of the road. Their silvery uniforms and broad-brimmed Smokey Bear hats were immaculate. I could almost hear their eyes track me as I walked down the road. I smiled, said "hi" and kept walking. Near the end of the formation, I paused to talk to the lone Black patrolman, easily the biggest cop I'd ever seen. I pegged him at 6'6" and 285 pounds. I introduced myself as a freelance reporter. He stared straight ahead, not responding.

"I'm writing an article about the rally and would like to ask you some questions," I said. Still no response. "Are you worried about what's going to happen?"

He turned his head a fraction of an inch toward me. "Um, ma'am. I'm here with my brothers," he said, nodding to the other cops. "So, we're not worried. We're here to protect their right to free speech. I can't say I'm real happy about having the North Carolinians here. They're troublemakers."

"Can we talk after the rally?" Officer Thaddeus Earle gave me his information and resumed his position.

I trudged up to the barn where two more goons in camo stood sentry. I hate camo. To me, camo means conformity and blind obedience. Instead of saying hello, one of them cocked an eyebrow at me.

"I'm looking for the head guys," I said. "I'm writing a story about the rally. I'm a freelance journalist."

They exchanged looks and the eyebrow cocker went inside. I glanced around while waiting to be admitted. The rally site was an empty cornfield with a 25-foot high, wooden cross smack in the middle. It could as easily have been a church re-treat as a Klan rally. Off to the left, a group of men surrounded a 55-gallon drum-turned-smoker still attached to the back of a pickup truck. My mouth watered at the smell of barbecue.

Eyebrow returned. "C'mon in. The Grand Dragon will see you," he said.

I followed him into the barn, which stank faintly of cow dung. Empty stalls stood on either side of the open space. In the middle, a fat man in khakis sat at a makeshift table made of old doors and sawhorses. A Styrofoam cup of coffee perched at his elbow. A white robe hung from some nearby rafters. Laid out on the table was a map of the southeastern states.

"Once we raise the cash, we can buy a nice plot of land

around here," said another man in camo, pointing to a spot west of Columbia. "That's where we'll do our training." Eyebrow, one pace in front of me, cleared his throat.

"S'cuze me, sirs. You have company," he said.

"Walter, you take this. I've got things to do," he said, stalking away from the table.

The bald man introduced himself as Walter Sparks, Columbia's Grand Titan.

"And that fellow was Glenn Miller, head of the North Carolina group that's putting on this shindig," he said.

He caught me eyeing his potbelly and smiled.

"Bought and paid for," he said, slapping his stomach. I chuckled politely.

"Well, little lady, what can I do you for?" he asked.

"I'd like to interview you for a story about the rally and about the recruiting that's going on," I replied, willing myself to be calm.

"Who did you say you're writing for?" Sparks asked, leaning back in his chair crossing his fingers over his stomach. My miniskirt was not doing its job.

"I didn't say. My plan is to write it and then find a place to publish it."

"Before we speak, I'd like to know which side you're on. I mean, what kind of article can we expect?" he asked, searching my face for clues.

"I'm not on anybody's side," I said. "My job is to give equal time to both sides and let the reader decide."

"So, you think of yourself as an impartial observer?" he asked, reaching for his coffee. "Where were you raised if I might ask."

"My dad was in the military so I was raised all over the place: Japan, Germany, Kansas, Virginia."

Sparks brightened. "Virginia, that's a good southern state."

"Now I live in Columbia," I said. "There's something about the South that gets under your skin." He nodded in agreement.

Eyebrow knocked on the door.

"Sir, Miller wants you out here," he said.

He looked over, "You can follow me around if you want, ask your questions while we walk." He moved fast, surprisingly fast for such a butterball.

"I don't know what you've heard about us, but we're good Christian people focused on community service," Sparks said. "We help people who need help." I adjusted my poker face.

"Last year, we raised funds for four scholarships to the University of South Carolina. "And before you ask, the recipients are the sons and daughters of our members," he said. I noticed he didn't say Klan.

"So, all the scholarships go to White kids?" I asked.

"Well, yes. But there's a lot of White kids who need this money as much as Black kids. They deserve to go to school too." He puffed up his chest.

I backed off. "Absolutely true. College loans can suck you dry before you even start working," I said.

Over his shoulder, I saw pickups and Broncos filling the parking area. Their occupants, all wearing baseball caps, bee-lined to the smoker and filled their plates. My stomach rumbled.

Miller jumped on to a makeshift platform. If it hadn't been for his permanent scowl and reputation for violence, I would've said he was attractive. He had a wiry build with high cheekbones and a big brown mustache. He dressed entirely in camouflage and on his head he wore a dark beret emblazoned with a cross.

"Folks, we're going to get started in about 45 minutes. In the meantime, help yourself to some barbeque. Enjoy yourselves!"

He waved Sparks over.

"Who's she?" Miller asked, eyeing me.

"She's writing a story about the rally. She's alright," Sparks reassured him.

Miller glared at Sparks and walked away.

"Wait. Did you need me?" he asked Miller's retreating back.

I followed Sparks over to the line of cops. "You're more than welcome to chow down," he said to the officers. "And you can bring him a plate too," he gestured to Officer Earle in what he supposed was an act of generosity. The officers declined.

"Suit yourselves," Sparks said, walking back toward the cross. "Stubborn sons a' bitches. I know most of their daddies and granddaddies," he said.

Remembering I was there, he added, "That's why we re-invented ourselves." I asked if I could take his photo next to the cross. He agreed but said he didn't want to wear his robe and hood. I snapped a few shots and asked some more questions, inching closer to dangerous topics.

"You mentioned the scholarships and community service. I was wondering though, does the Klan still have a problem with Black people and Jews?" I asked with as much innocence as I could pump into my voice.

"Well, I'd say we've learned to live side-by-side with not too much friction," Sparks responded.

"How'd you get involved in the Klan in the first place?" I asked. He winced at my use of the K word.

"This is a legacy organization whose membership is passed from generation to generation," he said. "My family has been in this group for a long time."

"How'd you get to be the Grand Titan?" I ventured.

"You have to be an upstanding member of the community, which I am. I own a car dealership on the outskirts of town. You ever need a car, give me a jingle," he said, winking. "I'll make you a good deal as long as I like the article you write."

"So, what else makes you a Grand Titan?" I asked.

He demurred, "You ever heard of the Freemasons? Our organization is secret like that. There's a lot of, you know, tests and handshakes and such that you have to know before you're permitted to wear the robe," he said.

"You keeping calling yourselves an organization. Do you ever call yourselves the KKK or the Klan anymore or is that out of date?" I asked.

"Well, amongst ourselves we do, but the name got a bad reputation, with all the lynchings way back in the day," he responded. Then he sucked in some air and looked abashed. He hadn't meant to talk about lynchings.

"You ever see a lynching?" I asked. He looked startled.

"Heavens no. Last one in South Carolina was almost 40 years ago. Those kinds of things don't happen here anymore. But my grandpa, actually both my grandpas, saw one." I asked him to tell me about it.

"Remember this was a long time ago. A Black family had just moved into a White part of town. They'd been warned that they weren't welcome – gently at first – you know, phone calls. But they didn't listen so things got more intense. Someone threw a brick through their front window. But they wouldn't go. So things hotted up," he said.

"A group got together and decided to burn a cross on their front lawn. The man made the mistake of coming out on the front porch with a shotgun. I think he was just threatening people – wouldn't've shot anyone, but one of our guys had his own gun and popped him in the leg and then all hell broke loose. Meantime, his wife was on the phone calling the sheriff. Funny thing was, the sheriff was out front setting up the cross. They dragged him out into the country and strung him up, or so I was told."

"And the sheriff didn't try to stop it?" I said.

"Like I said, it was a long time ago," he responded, shaking his head. "The only reason I joined was because my daddy joined and his daddy and on and on and on. It's tradition, like the rebel flag," he said. As he spoke, the sun started setting. A lovely pink color peeked through the trees. He excused himself and told me to get some food and enjoy the proceedings. As good as it smelled, I had a policy of never eating my enemy's food. I tried to interview some of the men who were chowing down, but no one was willing to go on the record.

"Y'all gather round," Miller blared through a red bullhorn. Walter scurried to the barn to retrieve his costume.

Miller's flunkies removed the ladder they'd used to reach the top of the cross. They had soaked it in kerosene. A group of men, still holding plates of barbecue, started moving to the area in front of the cross. I snapped a few shots.

"Now, I'm here to tell you about reality, ladies and gentlemen," Miller said. I looked around but saw no other women.

"The reality is that America is being overtaken by Jews, spics and bubble-lipped niggers," he said, pausing for effect. Now in a robe and peaked hood, Sparks stiffened at Miller's words, but he didn't look back at me.

"You know why it's happening," he asked. "It's because of birth control. White people are using it and Black people and spics ain't. What they're doing is fornicating like rabbits. Guess what? We're paying the bill. We're paying for welfare and food stamps for niggers and spics to make more little niggers and spics," he paused and looked at the audience.

"Yes, they're cute when they're little. But once they grow up, they want free everything. They want to suckle on the big pig's tit. Am I right?" he asked the crowd. The men mumbled their assent.

"Am I right?" he asked louder this time. Poked by his goons, a few hollered in agreement. "If they don't want welfare, they want our jobs and that's just as bad. How's a White family supposed to live, paying all these taxes to support them, and can't even get a decent job."

I looked over at Sparks who had jutted his chin out. The Black cop's face had hardened. I took a photo of Sparks with Officer Earle seething in the background.

"This here is a Christian nation founded on Christian principles," Miller said. "A Christian nation of White people. We didn't ask them to come here, but here they are. We need to make damn sure they know their place. And that place is below me and you." A few in the crowd started shouting out, "That's right. Tell them!"

Miller pulled out a Zippo lighter and lit an oily rag that was tied to the cross. The flames sprinted up and spread sideways on the cross pieces. This was the piece of drama the crowd had come to see. He held the still-flickering lighter over his head like he was at a rock concert and bellowed, "White power! White people shall inherit the earth. These black-as-night niggers and spics work for us. God made us, not them, in his image. White men rule the world. So it has been and so it shall remain."

The flames danced across 50 pairs of eyes. I moved closer and shot a picture of Miller with spittle on his chin and a twisted look in his eyes.

I'd never heard anything like the pure evil spouted at the rally. Did they believe this man's invective? Where was the kinder, gentler Klan that Sparks had described?

"Walter?" I called to him in the crowd. He shook his head and walked away from me. I went to the giant officer and began to pull out my notebook.

"I can't talk," he said under his breath. "If something's

going to happen, it'll happen now while people are riled up. If you're smart, you'll get on out of here."

The mood had shifted from that of a happy barbecue with the guys to something else. Anger that preyed on blue-collar fears seemed to be taking hold. I shot a few more photos and headed back to my car. Just as I put the key in the lock, I felt a hard hand clamp my elbow.

"You write anything that makes us look bad and you'll regret it," Miller snarled. "You hear me? In fact, I want to see what you write before you publish it. You can fax it to me here," he said, handing me a business card.

"Sure, I'll be happy to do that," I lied, anxious to make my getaway. No self-respecting journalist would give a source a look-see before publication. It was against the code.

I pulled out slowly to avoid drawing more attention to myself. Eyebrow pushed his cap to the back of his head as he watched me leave. With trembling fingers, I navigated back to the main road.

I flashed on my best pal, Connie, and the most popular kids in my high school, most of whom were Black. I was angry they had to live in a world with people like Glenn Miller and Walter Sparks not to mention their followers. My hand shook as I switched on the radio for music that might calm me. Blue Suede Shoes rocked me through the night to Columbia and the Black News where Tyrell was waiting.

"It was as bad as you thought it would be," I said, describing some of what I'd seen.

"Did they have any luck recruiting people?" he asked.

"I didn't get the feeling that the locals were happy with the North Carolinians telling them what to do. They're tripping all over themselves trying to make themselves out to be a community organization."

"Community organization, my eye," Tyrell said. "Let me tell you about Glenn Miller." After leaving the Green Berets, Miller had become the leader in a pro-Nazi party. They weren't aggressive enough for him, so he started the Carolina KKK to create an all-White nation that would link North and South Carolina.

"That's what he's trying to do. He wants to establish an all-White enclave – a million square miles—and call it Southland," he said, breaking off to look through a pile of clippings. He found one and passed it to me.

"Glenn says that 90 percent of murders are committed by Blacks and that's why Whites should always be armed. It's the combination of his military training and the KKK that worries me and a lot of other people. Right now, he trains these yokels at his farm." A jolt of fear spiked through me.

"He was talking to the local Klan chief about buying land around here for a training camp," I said. "He also threatened me if I wrote anything he didn't like."

Tyrell nodded, concern shadowing his features.

"I knew this assignment was risky when I took it," I said, quickly. "I'll be careful."

"Let me think about how we can provide you some protection," he said.

"I appreciate the offer, but I can't risk blowing my cover at camp. I'll watch my step."

After we worked out my deadline for the article, I headed to the darkroom. It was after midnight by the time I finished developing the film. I hung the wet strips to dry in the cabinet and made a mental note to follow up with the Black cop from the rally.

Chapter 24

MOHAWKED

I was bleary and anxious the next day but sleeping in wasn't an option. I had an eleven o'clock date with destiny at Hair Circus. In my past lives, I'd had a variety of buzz cuts so getting a mohawk shouldn't have been a big deal. But I worried about Moolah's reaction to my new look. Would she finally start booking me or would she punish me by extending my training beyond the six painful months I'd already endured?

I shook off my worry and went through my morning ablutions. At 10, I added ice to a cooler full of orange juice, plastic cups, and Cordon Negro, my favorite cheap bubbly. At the gate, I stopped to pick up Giselle, Billie, and Brandy and headed downtown.

Giselle and Billie volunteered to carry the cooler between them, and we climbed the narrow stairs to the salon. I flashed on the four of us approaching a wrestling ring to the roar of screaming hoards. Joan Jett's Bad Reputation played in my mind's soundtrack.

Instead of cheering and booing crowds at the top of the stairs, a receptionist in a dark bob and scarlet lips perched at her clear Lucite desk. In the middle of her telling me that

Raquel was with a customer, she poked her head around the partition and promised to be with us in "two ticks, hon."

We made ourselves at home in the lounge, popping open the first bottle of champers and pouring ourselves libations.

"Here's to your mohawk," Giselle toasted. "You are going to start raking in the dough, my friend."

We sipped our mimosas and settled in to wait. I carefully pulled out the comic Keith had lent me and once again examined the superhero I would soon become.

"I like her clothes," Brandy said, looking over my shoulder. "They're kind of a cross between a biker and a rocker. The good thing about biker gear is that it's really tough. It'll last forever."

The clack of Raquel's high-heeled boots announced her arrival. Then we caught sight of her black velvet corset under a sheer midnight blue top and black leather pants. All of us started hooting at her eye-catching get up.

"Well, hello to you too," she said, smiling and eyeing the bottle. I introduced her to my friends and she went up to each one and shook hands. I could see her assessing their hair, wanting to reach out and run her fingers through it. Billie and Brandy both had luxurious manes, untouched by chemicals. Giselle, on the other hand, barely combed her short blonde curls.

"I love your photos," Giselle gushed, holding onto Raquel's hand for a few extra beats. Billie bristled a little. Was Giselle flirting with her?

"Bit of the bubbly?" I offered, reaching for the bottle, but she declined.

"I'd love one," she said. "Hair of the dog and all that. But I'd hate myself if I got tipsy and messed up your mohawk. First things first."

"Save me a glass," she said, reaching out and running her fingers through my hair.

"I'll do better than that. I'll save you two."

"Do you have a picture of what you'd like?" she asked.

I showed her Keith's comic. "I want to look like her." I thought she might laugh because I was showing her a cartoon, but she took it seriously.

"It's going to look great on you. But, like I told you, your hair is so straight I'm going to have to perm it to get it to stand up like you want," she said.

She stood and pointed to the closest salon chair. Two smiling stylists peered over to see what the hubbub was about.

"You're really sure about this?" she said, giving me a good hard look. I took a gulp of my drink and nodded. "This is a small town and people are going to stare. You okay with that?"

"People have always stared at me. I don't care," I said.

She whipped out a black plastic smock and floated it down around my shoulders. After securing it at the neck, she combed my paltry locks. I took a big sip of champagne. My heart fluttered. I was getting a little nervous. Billie opened the second bottle and poured another round. Sweat beaded on my upper lip. I wiped it off with the back of my hand.

Raquel ran a part down the right side of my head and clipped it up. She did the same on the left side and then went to her drawer of medieval-looking tools and implements. Suddenly she turned, clenching an electric hair trimmer high in her right hand.

"Are you ready?" she asked, looking over my head in the mirror.

My pulse was racing and the color drained from my face. I was accustomed to people staring at me because of my height and wondered if it would be any worse than that.

Giselle must have sensed my trepidation and proposed another toast. "To fame, fortune, and the championship belt. To Pippi!"

Billie and Brandy lifted their glasses and shouted, "To Pippi!" By now, the other stylists had gathered round.

I downed my drink and nodded to Raquel.

"Go for it," I said. Giselle, Billie, and Brandy cheered.

Raquel gave me a mock evil look and flipped the "on" switch. The high whine of the trimmer sounded alarmingly like a dental drill. Starting above my right ear, she ran the trimmer along my scalp. Strands of hair fell to my shoulders. It reminded me of mowing an overgrown lawn. My friends gathered around me and stared at the section of newly bared scalp. I could feel a cool breeze from the air conditioner on this virgin territory.

Brandy reached out and touched it. "It feels like beard stubble," she said.

"That's right," Raquel said. "We'll razor off the stubble when we're done with the cut and perm. That way, the chemicals won't burn your head as much."

My friends refilled their glasses and continued to watch me. Raquel ran the trimmer over the next row and a thicker clump of hair fell. Again and again, she ran the trimmer through my hair, leaving stubble behind. Pretty soon, all that remained was a three-inch wide strip of hair down the center of my head.

"I like it!" Giselle said, passing me a full glass of bubbly.

The cut was the first step. Raquel pulled out some white perming rods. One of the other stylists rolled over a table with all the accouterments needed for a perm. She curled a row down my remaining hair in less than 15 minutes. She added long pieces of cotton around my hairline to keep me from getting burned by the evil-smelling chemicals. The bubbly and adrenaline were making me loopy.

Once she added the chemicals, Raquel let out a big sigh and relaxed. She accepted a glass of champagne. I invited the other stylists to help us work on the third bottle.

"I love the name of your place," I told Raquel. "How'd you come up with Hair Circus?"

"You're not going to believe this, but I wanted to be in the circus when I was a kid," she said, leaning back in a nearby salon chair. "I learned gymnastics and was pretty good. I figured I could be the girl doing tricks on horseback or maybe on the trapeze. I didn't care what I did as long as I was in the circus." She took a long sip of wine.

"My mom and dad sat me down and had a serious talk with me when I was about 13. We'd gone to see the circus and I'd been talking their ears off about joining up when I was old enough. They were gentle, but they laid it out for me. I wasn't ever going to be in the circus. I needed to find a way to make a living. It broke my heart."

The stink of the chemicals squatted under my nose and I blew a breath out.

"That's so sad," I said. "Do you ever regret not giving it a try?"

She smiled and sipped her drink. "You know, I did while I was in high school. But then I got bitten by the beauty bug." She pushed an errant strand of hair from her eyes. "There were many times when the salon owner I was working for treated me like dirt, and I thought about leaving all this behind. Throw caution to the wind."

Her bustier was starting to droop and she tugged it up. "But I never did. I was too scared to start something new and I was too comfortable here in my hometown. Plus, my grandma got sick and needed help. I couldn't leave my family behind. I'm at peace with my choice."

The timer chimed and Raquel put a towel around my shoulders and walked me to the basin. She and one of her assistants pulled out the curlers and dropped them in a green basket. The hair sprang into nickel-sized ringlets. She washed out my remaining hair with warm water and ran her fingers through my curls. She gently massaged my scalp reddened by the strong chemicals. I closed my eyes and sighed.

She spread cool foam on the sides of my head and, with a few swipes of the straight razor, removed the stubble. Virgin skin that hadn't seen the light of day since I was an infant glowed like moonstone. The skin was silky soft and the air over my shaved scalp was the strangest sensation. Cold, slightly damp and tingly: it felt like freedom.

The next step was to tease and taunt the tuft of curls into a stand-at-attention mohawk. It took no more than 10 minutes and half a can of hairspray to make my hair stand straight up. All my nervousness was gone, replaced by pure joy. I turned around in the mirror, loving what I saw.

Brandy asked if she could do my makeup. She gave me long Spock-like eyebrows with a pencil, applied eyeliner to give me cat eyes, and handed me a ruby red lipstick. I put on my earrings and turned back toward the mirror. I'd been transformed into a different person than the plain Jane who'd walked into the salon hours before.

"Yours is, by far, the wildest cut I've ever done. Remember you promised me a photo for my salon." Raquel handed me her photographer's number on a slip of paper.

Just then, the door downstairs opened and someone began climbing the stairs. We all turned to see a tall man filling the doorway. He was at least 6'4", his form-fitting black T-shirt and jeans accentuating wide shoulders and a whittled waist. Tucked under his arm was a skull-topped motorcycle helmet and across his shoulder, leather saddlebags. He looked like a young Hemingway. The motor in my pants started revving.

"Well, speak of the devil, here's Ron," Raquel said, walking toward him with open arms. "I was just giving Pippi your phone number."

I was a little drunk and my hormones were howling. I saw Ron and all I wanted to do was rip his clothes off.

Since that wasn't an option, I walked right up and said, "Hi Ron, you great big hunk of a man. I'm Pippi. Wanna take my picture?"

He threw his head back and guffawed. After he caught his breath, I introduced him to the girls. I could see he was intrigued by Brandy and Giselle.

Ron clicked off half a dozen Polaroids of me right there in the waiting room. We made plans to get together in the next few weeks. With Raquel's help, we killed the fourth bottle of cava and it was time to go. Raquel told us to keep in touch, let her know how we were doing. I wasn't sober enough to drive so I passed the keys to Billie, who had stopped drinking earlier.

At the gate to the compound, I scrunched down in the seat. I wasn't ready to confront the evil queen. Would Moolah throw me out? Would she yell and scream? Giselle and the rest of them got out at her place and I slipped across the seat to drive the last bit toward my house.

Wolfgang was sitting on his front steps buffing his rifle, when I drove up. Few things look more masturbatory than a man polishing the long hard barrel of a shotgun. I didn't see a beer next to him, so I counted that on the plus side.

I put the car into park and held on to the steering wheel. I took a deep breath. If he saw me, I was pretty sure that he'd tell his girlfriend who'd tell Moolah. The grapevine would buzz with the news. But then I figured it was going to happen no matter what. Out of the corner of my eye, I could see him peering at me, trying to figure out why I was sitting in my car. I got out and walked over to him.

"Hi, Wolfgang. How's it going?" His jaw dropped when he saw me. He didn't say anything, just gaped at my new do.

"What? You don't like it?" He still didn't say anything. I didn't need this. I turned on my heel and began walking back toward my house.

"You have really screwed the pooch this time," he said. "Bet you didn't ask Moolah. Too late now."

"What do you mean?" I asked, turning back around. "I think it looks great."

He shook his head. "It's not very feminine. Guys aren't going to like it," he said.

"Screw feminine, screw guys. I'm tough," I said, flexing a bicep.

He looked over my shoulder and whispered, "Don't move."

I almost balked, thinking he was still razzing me. But in his voice was the same tone I'd heard when I'd been swimming with a friend in Tampa Bay and gotten swarmed by sharks.

A rattling sound made the newly permed hair on the back of my neck stand up. I held my breath and squeezed my eyes shut. Slowly, Wolfgang lifted his rifle to his shoulder and aimed. Wait? Was he aiming at me? I squeezed my eyes shut and a shot rang out so loud my ears rang.

"What the hell?" I began, and he turned me around by my shoulder. Three feet from where I stood, within striking distance of my bare leg, was a large rattlesnake. Wolfgang had blown the head from the body. He reached out to pick it up and I yanked his arm away.

"Don't touch the head. It can still bite you."

He looked around and found a shovel next to the side of the house. He dug a hole, dropped the snakehead in, and covered it with dirt. "Satisfied?" he asked. He reached for the rest of the snake. It was a big boy, four inches around.

"What on earth are you going to do with it?"

First, he said, he was going to skin it for a hatband and then he was going to barbecue it for dinner.

"Seeing as how it almost bit you, you should come over for dinner and bite it back," he said.

"You sure Crystal won't mind? We're not exactly close."

"Don't you worry about her. She'll be fine. Plus, she's going to want to see that new haircut of yours," he grinned.

I really didn't want to like this guy, but he was starting to grow on me. He headed back to his place, his rifle in one hand and the snake in the other.

"Hey, Wolfgang?" I called. He turned and looked at me with raised eyebrows.

"Thanks. You saved my ass."

"Don't worry about it," he said. "Seven o'clock? Bring beer. Lots of beer." I nodded and went home. I drank down a glass of tepid tap water, leaning against the counter. The wine and adrenaline had caught up with me. I barely made it to my bed and would've slept all night if I hadn't gotten the whiff of something delicious wafting through the window.

I dragged myself to the shower, but couldn't fit a shower cap over my mohawk. I leaned my head back to keep it dry. I threw on some cutoffs and a tank top, grabbed a couple of six-packs, and headed next door. Wolfgang was standing at the grill with a long fork in his hand. He smiled and pointed at the body of the snake curled in the middle of the smoking grill.

"It smells incredible," I said. "Was it hard to gut?" I handed him a beer and grabbed one for myself.

"Nah. After you pull off the skin, you slice it down the belly and pull out the innards. Not hard at all," he said. Crystal stood at the top of their stairs. I wondered what she was going to say. She smirked and shook her head. It was a better reaction than I'd expected, seeing as how she'd never actually addressed me directly before.

"I'm trying to get Moolah off the dime and book my first match," I said.

"I guess you've been training long enough," she said. "Want me to put that in the fridge?"

I passed her the beer and rejoined Wolfgang who described in detail how to tan a snakeskin. We chowed down after a few beers. The stringy meat tasted like payback.

Crystal turned out to be really nice, just a little shy. I'd totally misread her. I still wondered if she'd out me to Moolah.

Chapter 25

THE BIG BOOT

The next morning, I was so nervous my scalp prickled. I smooshed a red bandana over my new mohawk. By now, I was pretty sure everyone, including Linda, knew that I'd cut my hair but the bandana would give her the option of ignoring it. That's what she did.

One slit-eyed glance at me and Linda announced, "Today we're going to put some moves together like you do in a real match." Had she read my mind?

"Okay, gather round," Linda said. "We're going to start out with a simple combination and then work up from there. I want you to throw your partner into the ropes and clothesline her. Make sure you're close to the ropes when you start, so your partner has enough room to hit the ropes on the opposite side. Then, I want you to pull her up by her hair and put her into a wristlock. Work that for a minute and then go into a body slam. Then I want you to drop a big leg across her neck."

She reviewed the moves one more time. Hit the ropes, a clothesline, a wristlock, a body slam, and finally a leg drop.

"Five moves in all. Think you can manage that?" she asked, looking at each one of us. We nodded. She demonstrated the moves with Giselle. It was a thing of beauty, one move flowing smoothly into another.

"Okay Stretch, you're up."

Instead of a clothesline, she instructed me to give my opponent the big boot. "You stick your leg up at chest height and let her run into it," Linda said. "This is a great move for someone with big feet like you. Now remember, you're not kicking her, you're letting her run into your foot."

I threw Giselle into the ropes and she ran straight into my boot. She guided my foot so she would control the impact. She took a beautiful bump backward and I grabbed her up by the hair and then moved into a wristlock. I reached down and hooked my elbow under her crotch for a body slam followed by the leg drop. It wasn't as smooth as Giselle's set, but it wasn't half bad. No one but me did the boot. Maybe it was going to be my signature move.

We kept working this set of moves again and again until we'd memorized the sequence like a bunch of dance steps. Everyone was in a good mood by the end of practice.

"Stretch, stay behind for a minute," Linda said as I got ready to scoot out of the ring. The other girls shot me glances as they were leaving.

"Shut the door behind you," Linda told Giselle.

She turned to me. "I heard you cut your hair." She reached over and yanked off my bandana. My mohawk looked a mess. It was full of hair spray and mashed down. I'm sure I looked like I was wearing a dead cat on my head. I reached up to touch the matted strands.

"It's a lot better when it's standing up," I said.

"For your sake, I hope so," she said. "Moolah wants to see you at 1:30."

"What about? Is she mad?"

I was scared of Linda but much more scared of Moolah.

"Guess you'll find out," Linda said.

I called Dave to let him know I wouldn't be able to make my shift. It was the first time I'd missed work and he was nice about it. My stomach rumbled but I was too nervous to eat anything more than a couple of crackers. I decided to try to mimic Storm's biker look in this first presentation to Moolah.

After fluffing up my mohawk, I pulled on tight black jeans and a black tank. I accessorized with my handcuff earrings, cowboy boots, and a giant brass belt that looked a little like a championship belt. I carefully applied makeup, less heavy-handed than Brandy's application, but following the same pattern. I took one last look and decided I was ready. Wolfgang and Crystal were getting into their car as I left my house.

"Looking good!" Wolfgang called.

"Good luck!" Crystal said, waving. I guessed they knew what was going down. At 1:25, I walked down the lake road, cold water running through my veins. The deed was done though and I had to own this.

Darlene was keeping a look-out for me from her child-sized lawn chair outside of Moolah's door. As usual, she scowled when she saw me but didn't say anything. She hopped up and ushered me inside.

Moolah was sitting on her couch, flipping through a magazine. She was going for the movie-star-at-home look in a full-length, zebra-pattered caftan, a gold tassel dangling from her bosom. The ensemble was set off by clanking gold bangles, heavy eyeliner, and a wall of perfume. In her twenties, she had been a valet known as "Slave Girl" wearing a short, leopard tunic and a tiger-tooth necklace.

Moolah did a double-take and I struck a pose. I widened my stance, arms akimbo, and hit her with my best sexy scowl.

Giselle and I had practiced in the bathroom mirror and I was ready. I am powerful and fierce. Powerful and fierce was my mantra as I waited for her response.

She tossed her magazine on the table and stood to get a better look. She reached out, took my hands, and spread them wide.

"Well, aren't you something," she said in a voice that was neither pleased nor angry. "Turn around." I twirled, feeling as clumsy as a dancing bear.

"Well, I'll be. I don't think I've seen anything this outlandish since I wrestled Bald Lady Angel," Moolah said. "You ever heard of her? Course you haven't. She was big like you and bald as a cue ball. Oowhee was she ugly, but she could draw the crowds."

Moolah paused to pick something out of her teeth. "Now, why did you want to go and cut your hair like that? You must've noticed that all my girls have long hair."

A plummeting feeling went through me as though I was falling off a tall building. I went ahead and leaped.

"I saw a comic book character with a mohawk. I thought it would make a good wrestling gimmick." I used Wolfgang's word, which I was pretty sure was the right one to describe my costume. Moolah raised an eyebrow at me.

"Plus, there was a guy with a mohawk in those Mad Max movies. They're my favorite. You know, with Mel Gibson." She didn't say anything so I laid my cards on the table. "I thought if I showed you how cool I can look, you might start booking me. I need to make some money."

She snorted. "Sugar, you sound just like me when I was getting started." She narrowed her eyes. "Now, I wouldn't have chosen a mohawk. Makes you look mannish, but it's done, and we'll do what we can with it." She frowned at me.

I self-consciously smoothed my hand over the whitewalls of my head.

"You need a name ..." she began.

I'd heard of wrestlers getting saddled with horrible names so I jumped in. "I was thinking about Mad Maxine," I said. "For when I'm a heel. And Lady Maxine for when I'm a babyface." I held my breath. I probably wasn't supposed to know those terms yet.

"Not bad." She nodded her head. "That might work."

"As far as clothes go, you're going to need a leotard," she said. "The jeans won't work in the ring. And you're going to need some wrestling boots," Moolah said. "We're going to get you ready for your first match. What do you think about that?"

"Yes!" I said. "I can't wait to start learning how to string all the moves together and start working."

"Don't you worry about that. I'm going to take over your training from here on. Listen to me and you'll be fine," Moolah said.

"So, you're not mad about the mohawk?" I asked. I knew I was pressing my luck, but still wanted her to tell me I'd done a good thing.

She reached out to run her fingertips across my smooth scalp. Without warning, she grabbed my earlobe and yanked me down to face level. It hurt like hell and I wondered if she'd ripped my earring off.

"I'm not mad, darling," she said. "But don't go making any other decisions without talking to me first. You belong to me now. The sooner you have that straight, the happier we'll all be." She smiled and sat back down. Darlene pushed me out the door.

Outside, I wanted to jump and scream for joy, but I played it cool in case anyone was watching. I was busting to tell someone, so I headed over to Giselle's. I never stopped to consider that she might not be overjoyed for me.

"Seriously, Moolah said she's going to start training you herself?"

Her face flushed pink, then red.

"That's not fair," she sputtered. "I've been here a lot longer than you and I'm a better wrestler than you."

"Everyone's a better wrestler than me," I said. "Well, except Brandy and maybe Wanda. The only reason Moolah's doing it is because of the mohawk. She thinks she can make some money."

But Giselle wasn't listening.

"I'm happy for you, Pippi. I am. But I'm not going to be left behind by someone who started training after me."

She stalked off, leaving me standing in her living room. The front door slammed and I went outside to watch her march over to Moolah's house. Darlene was there, guarding the front door as usual. They argued. Darlene shook her head "no." Giselle tried to push past her, but Darlene grabbed onto her right calf and sat on her foot. Giselle tried to shake her off, but Darlene was tenacious. Behind them, Moolah pushed open the screen door. Darlene let go and Giselle slipped inside.

The next morning, when I was handing her a cafe con leche, Linda told me I'd be skipping the afternoon practice. She came closer, "You'll be working out with the old faces. This is just for you. You don't share anything you learn with the other new faces."

"Shouldn't everyone know how to wrestle for real?" I asked. "Isn't that why we're here?"

"You have any problems with the rules, you take it up with management," she said, nodding toward the mansion. She knocked into my shoulder on her way to the ring.

Chapter 26

LEARNING TO SELL

After the first practice, I headed home to shower. I thought I'd celebrate a free afternoon by heading to Keith's for some afternoon delight. A few orgasms would loosen me up for the evening's practice, I thought. I was humming in the shower, whistling while I put on my prettiest panties.

But Keith's car wasn't in the driveway. I retrieved his key from under a loose brick and let myself in. On the kitchen counter, he'd left a note saying that he'd had to go home to deal with a family emergency. He didn't say when he'd be back.

I made myself comfortable, first taking off my bra, then putting on Keith's robe and flopping on the couch. I wanted to tell someone who'd actually be happy for me but Connie was working. I called Joann, who worked for herself. She picked up on the third ring.

"It's finally happening, Joann. Moolah's going to start training me for my first match." I told her about joining the old faces' practice and Giselle's negative reaction.

"Don't worry about Giselle," Joann said. "She'll come around. Her feelings are probably hurt. She needs a chance to realize it's not your fault."

"You and Chuck should come up to visit me," I said. "I'll take you to Group Therapy, that bar I told you about. Maybe we'll stage a catfight in your honor. You can meet Keith, the guy I'm seeing. I think you'll like him. He's really nice."

She promised she'd talk to Chuck and we said our goodbyes. A visit from Joann would be a balm to my soul.

While I waited for Keith, I ate a turkey sandwich. I washed my hands and settled down with some X-men comics, featuring Storm, of course. The tryptophan in the turkey hit me hard and I felt myself nodding off. I forced myself to set an alarm. I couldn't risk being late to the first practice with Moolah.

I felt better after my nap, but I was hyperaware of the clock ticking me closer to destiny. I shucked Keith's robe and did some naked yoga. After a dozen sun salutations, it was time to return to camp.

I left Keith a note that I'd been by and let him know I'd made a long-distance call and would repay him. I didn't think he'd worry about such a piddling thing but didn't want to take advantage. I changed into my workout clothes and headed back to camp at 6:30.

Some of the older girls had already gathered outside the workout ring. I drove past them to my place. Giselle was sitting at the top of my steps waiting for me. She walked over to my car and opened the door for me.

"I wanted you to know that I'm really happy for you," she said. "I really want you to start getting booked. This isn't about you, it's about me and Moolah. Anyway, I wanted to make sure we were cool." I laughed out loud.

"Of course we're cool," I said. "What did Moolah say? Did she agree to let you practice with us?"

"She told me to wait a couple of weeks so she can focus on your training. After that, it'll be my turn. She knows I want to be a heel like my Aunt Dominique and she says she's been thinking about that."

"Are you sure you can't crash practice?" I pleaded. "I really want you there."

"A little longer and I'll be in there with you. Anyway, Billie will be there so you will have at least one friend." I looked at my watch.

"Crap! I'm almost late," I said. "Gotta run." I hugged her before sprinting to the workout ring. "Thanks, Giselle." I called over my shoulder.

The veterans were already inside the training ring when I arrived. I was the last one in and Darlene shut the door behind me. I slid into the ring flat on my stomach and was getting up when someone shoved her boot next to my nose. I looked up and saw that it was attached to Zoey. I had tried to apologize again for the flying head scissors incident, but she was never going to like me. She was letting me know that I was in her territory and she didn't like it.

"You think you're ready to run with the big dogs?" she taunted. I shoved her foot away and tried to push into the ring. But she jammed her foot at my face again. Billie didn't say anything but stepped forward and reached out a hand to help me up. Good ol' Billie. I felt like sticking my tongue out at the punk.

"Stretch's with us today," Linda told the group. "Try to go easy." I heard a few mumbles and snorts.

"I'll be nice," Zoey said with a malicious smile.

"We're going to warm up with some hair pulling," Linda boomed. Some of the vets grumbled. "I know you think you know how to do this. But I want to see you sell it, work it. Make me believe." She gave the group instructions, but I could tell it was mostly for my benefit.

"The girl who goes first, reach over and grab two big handfuls of your partner's hair." She looked at me directly. "Grab hair that's in the middle of the head, not the front. It won't hurt as much. Now, the other girl, I want you to grab her wrists so that you control how hard she's pulling. We're going to do this slow at first."

She gestured for Zoey and Billie to stand in front of her. They knew the drill. Billie reached over and sank her hands into Zoey's curly black hair. Zoey grabbed Billie's wrists and they both leaned forward, preparing for battle.

"Billie, I want you to whipsaw her and make it look as painful as possible."

Billie pumped slightly to the right to let Zoey know what she was going to do. Then she yanked her to the left while Zoey gave a little off-balance kick, cried out, and grimaced. Billie paused, pushing down on her hands so she towered above the girl. "How do you like that," Billie taunted. "You want some more?"

Goose pimples covered my arms. In the ring, Billie was scary. She lifted Zoey by the hair and lashed her the other way, this time not pausing but going straight into another move, drawing her into a snaky formation.

All the while, Zoey stomped the ring, throwing one of her legs up and generally making faces like Billie was killing her. They performed the move a couple more times until Linda yelled, "Switch."

They swapped and Zoey grabbed hold of Billie's long locks. Billie grabbed Zoey's wrists and they went through the exercise. This time, though, Billie left one hand on Zoey's wrist and, with the other, attempted to gouge her opponent's throat and eyes. Whenever she did this, Zoey would give her an extra hard yank and bring her to heel like a bad dog.

After the demonstration, Linda told us to select a partner and practice the move, two couples at a time.

"Stretch, you're with Billie."

Billie walked over and gave me a long look. "Well, you don't have much hair so there's not much to grab. You have to really go with it when I pull. Think of it like a dance. Remember to grab ahold of my wrists."

"Take it easy on me, okay?" I said. "A thin strip of hair is all I have."

"Okay, let's go," Linda boomed. Billie gave me the pump signal and with a shocking amount of strength yanked me to the left. I hadn't been prepared for the force so my head snapped back. I caught up by the second yank and managed to regain my balance.

"Sell it, Stretch," Linda instructed. "Don't just stand there."

"What?" This wasn't something she'd taught us yet.

"Sell it," she repeated.

"I don't know how."

Linda stopped and looked at me. "Did you ever play pretend when you were a kid?" she said. "That's what you do. Pretend that Billie's hurting you."

This is the stuff I'd been begging to be taught.

"I'll try." I backed up and got into a wrestling stance.

Billie grabbed me by my hair and started pulling. I started screaming for her to "Get off of me, you bitch. I'm going to fucking kill you. Let me go right now."

I threw my head around and glowered at each move she made. Linda told Billie to stop and said, "What the hell was that?" I felt my face flush red.

"I was trying to sell it," I said in a whisper.

"Not like that," Linda said. "First of all, no cussing. This is family entertainment and you can't be cussing in front of little kids."

I snorted at the idea that beating the hell out of each other in a wrestling ring was considered family entertainment.

Billie teamed up with Zoey to show me what she meant.

Zoey lurched toward Billie and they went at each other like a clap of thunder. Billie got Zoey by her hair, but instead of screaming like me, Zoey grunted.

So, cussing was out and high-pitched yelling. I needed to bring my voice down into a lower register. Live and learn. I was going to have to practice. We worked on hair-pulling exercises for 15 minutes or so.

"Remember, turnabout is fair play. If you pull your opponent's hair, then she's going to do it to you," Linda said. Next, she instructed us to partner up to work on holds.

"I want to see you work and sell each hold until I say switch. Then, you'll swap and go into another hold and then another until I say stop." I was paired up with Billie again. Linda yelled, "Start!"

Billie grabbed my right wrist and slid under my arm, which was fully extended. As she moved, she slipped her hand around my wrist so it looked like she was wrenching my wrist. She began to work it and I pretended to get ready to make a move. She lifted up my wrist so it looked like she was inflicting greater harm. A few more pounds of torque and it really would have hurt. I did my best to sell the move and make it look super painful. Linda yelled, "switch" and I put Billie into a wristlock. I bent her arm at the elbow and tucked her wrist behind her neck. Again, she mimed that I was wrenching her wrist and arm. She was selling it so hard I thought I might be hurting her for real.

"Are you okay?" I whispered into her ear. She kept selling it and nodded her head once. Wow, she was good. She reversed the move again and yanked on my hair so I had to take a bump backward. Linda hadn't said we had to stand up while we were practicing these moves, so I guess it was okay. Billie pulled me up by the hair for another round of holds.

"Remember, you're going to use these holds to slow down a match or when you blow up and need to catch your breath," Linda said. "Okay, everybody warmed up now?

My heart sank. This was the warm-up? We'd been at it for half an hour. I thought we were already working out. As soon as that thought crossed my mind, the door flung open and Moolah entered. Or rather, she made an entrance.

She had squeezed herself into a black leotard and tights. Fat bulged above and below her too-tight waistband. She rolled into the ring. Linda offered Moolah a hand up but she ignored it and rocked up like the rest of us. The older girls buzzed around her but I stayed outside the circle.

Moolah thrust a sinewy arm through the thicket of women, grabbed the front of my shirt, and yanked me toward her. I couldn't help bumping into Zoey, who did not want to make room for me. "Sorry," I whispered from the wake of Moolah's tractor beam.

"How are my girls?" she said, smiling with her hand still on my shirt. Her fingernails were latched to the front of my bra and digging into my breasts.

"I'm glad to see y'all. Now, girls, this here is Pippi. She's been training with the new faces and I'm moving her up. She's new so I want y'all to help her all you can." She looked at each of the girls, her eyes resting a little longer on Zoey

"Her first match is in a couple of weeks, and you're going to help me get her ready," she said. I couldn't believe I'd heard right. Two weeks? My pulse hammered in my neck. This was much sooner than I'd thought.

"Everybody out of the ring except for Pippi."

Moolah snagged me around the neck and put me in a tight headlock. I balanced myself against her hips as she walked around the ring. Fused like Siamese twins, we walked from one turnbuckle to another. I did my best to follow her around the ring without stumbling.

"When I'm choking you, I want you to make it look like you are doing your best to break the hold," she instructed. "Act like I'm wearing you down, that you can't breathe. Slap my arm." She strode across the ring, dragging me behind her. If my neck weren't in her arm vise, it'd be kind of funny given our size difference. She had my skull tucked right up against her right side, her right breast sitting on my head like a jaunty beret. At first, she held me with one arm. Then she locked her hands and mimed that she was cutting off my air. She grabbed my hair and pulled me into a back bump.

"After I strangle you and I get you on the mat, don't get up and act like it was nothing," she said. "Stop to get your breath, hold your neck like it's injured. Take your time getting up."

She pulled me up by my hair and swiftly pumped her arms down-up-down into a flying mare. I did a nice bump onto my back and she followed me down with a stranglehold around my neck. My knees were bent and I stomped the mat. I reached back to grab her hair but she craned away and made out like she was strangling me even harder.

Moolah pulled me up by my mohawk again and smacked me across the upper chest. It stung like hell. I pictured the handprint on Jessica's chest at the Lion's Club match so many months ago. "The realer it looks, the more it hurts," she had said. I refocused on Moolah's instructions.

"Exaggerate your movements so someone sitting in the back row knows what you're doing," she said. "And when you smack your opponent, follow all the way through. Make it easy for your partner to sell what you're doing."

A little bit of pain was necessary to make the moves look real, she said. The pain of a slap, a punch, a hair pull, was fleeting and not worth noticing.

"Yell at the crowd, argue with the ref, stomp around the ring. The worst thing you can do is stand there like a lump. It brings down the crowd's energy."

She'd been smacking and yanking and strangling me for close to 20 minutes; I felt light-headed but surprisingly intact. She drove her fist into my hair and jerked my face toward hers. She blew her awful cinnamon gum and coffee breath on me.

Our eyes were inches away. Her orange lipstick had seeped into deep lip fissures. She gave me a long look that said, "I'm going to eat your liver. I'm going to chew it up and swallow it."

My bladder filled with cold water. I couldn't tell if she was really going to hurt me. She held me for another beat and shoved me toward Linda who leaped up from the turnbuckle and caught me like I was a small fish thrown overboard.

"Billie and Carmen, get up here," Moolah said.

I scooted out of the ring, heart thumping in my throat. The veterans took over and we all watched their battle dance, graceful and lethal looking. Their moves were seamless, moving from one to another. The pace varied, sometimes they moved at lightning speed, and other times they ground out moves, slow and painful. Billie and Carmen sold the moves, responding to the sound of slaps and punches. I watched them carefully, desperate to know what they knew, to move with such grace and viciousness.

Finally, it was over. I was almost empty, as tired and wrecked as the first time I'd gotten into the ring. There was so much to learn. Selling was a whole other element to think about on top of the moves. Maybe it made sense, I thought, to make us first learn the moves so they became automatic.

"Next practice is Thursday, 7 o'clock," Linda said and I limped home.

The next morning came too soon. My body was back to hurting like it had when I'd first started training. Giselle came over during first practice and shot me a questioning look. "Tell you later," I whispered, turning my attention to Linda.

"Today, kiddies, we're going to learn a different kind of the monkey flip," she said. "The main difference is that you land on your stomach, not on your back. Giselle, get over here."

All of us groaned. I hated belly bumps, which were the opposite of badass. Landing on your stomach made you look like a big stupid baby. And they left bruises on my hipbones and didn't feel so great on my boobs either. Brandy had it worse.

Without preamble, Linda reached down and grabbed Giselle behind the knees, fell backward, and catapulted Giselle over her head. For a second, she was airborne, her elbows bent and angled flat to the mat. She absorbed the main impact on her thighs, arms, and stomach.

We spent the next half hour soaring over each other's heads. The third time, Giselle looked down as she flew over my head and said, "Hey, Pippi." I laughed out loud, startled.

In line, she confided, "You know girls talk to each other when they're in the ring, tell each other the next moves. Sometimes they talk when they're flying. But never let anybody see or hear you under pain of death."

After practice, I called Dave and begged off the morning shift. I needed time to pound out a rough draft of the KKK article while the memories were still fresh.

"This is the second time you've called in," he said. "I don't mean to be a hard-ass but one more time and I'll have to look for someone new. I need someone dependable." I apologized again.

⚬⚬

After showering, I spread my notes on the kitchen table. I was still working out the lead paragraph when I heard a knock. I stood up so fast, my chair fell over. I threw my notebook onto the top shelf of my kitchen cabinet and answered the door.

Giselle and Billie stood there, arms slung across each other's shoulders.

"We heard the good news!" Billie said, smiling.

"Good news?" My mind was still on the article. And then I flashed on Moolah saying my first match was coming up in two weeks.

"Yeah, your first match," Billie said, high-fiving me. Giselle hopped on my back, yelling like a banshee. My reporter's notebook glowed like kryptonite from the shelf in the kitchen.

"Let's catch the breeze," I said, moving them outside. We settled on the top step.

"Did Linda tell you anything about your first match?" Giselle asked. "I heard you might be working with Wendi."

"Wendi Richter?" Billie and I both said, turning toward her.

"Yep, she's doing that deal with Cyndi Lauper," Giselle said. "Wendi's already defeated Moolah once. They're trying to keep the story going. You might be her secret weapon."

Billie's mood shifted from jubilant to angry. "Moolah talked to me about working with Wendi," she said. "What's she playing at?"

"Why didn't you tell me, Billie?" Giselle said.

"I didn't tell you because it's not real until the match is booked," Billie said. "It's more of Moolah's bullshit."

"I didn't know anything about this," I said, taking a deep breath and holding it.

"Maybe she's messing with you both," Giselle said. "Pitting you against each other so you have to compete for the same job."

"You've got to be the one who wrestles Wendi," I told Billie. "I'll tell her so."

"It's not up to you or me," Billie said. "She'll book whoever she wants. And then she'll take half our pay for doing almost nothing. I can't even pay my GD bills!"

"But what can we do?" Giselle said. "She's the biggest name in lady wrestling." We sat there, watching the ducks. Without thinking, Giselle started humming the song, "Girls Just Want to Have Fun."

"Can't we start our own group?" I said. "You, me and Billie." They started laughing at me.

"No, really. Why not? Billie, you know all the promoters, don't you? Can't we work with them ourselves? Plus, you're a fantastic heel." Billie leaned back on her elbows.

"With your blond curls, you'd be a great babyface, Giselle," I said.

"I'm not a fucking babyface," Giselle said, standing up and clomping to the bottom of the stairs. "I'm a heel, like my aunt."

"But fans would love it," I said, ignoring her protests. "They'd hate Billie for beating on you. With my height and mohawk, I guess I'd have to be a heel. If Brandy came with us, she could go either way. But she'd sell tickets no matter what."

"So, say we did something like this," Giselle said, slowly warming to the idea. "And I'm not saying we are. But if we did, how'd we go about it?"

I thought about it for a minute. "Well, I guess the first thing is to get new photos," I said. "I could makes us a brochure with the new photos and send them to promoters."

Giselle grinned. "You know how to do that?"

I nodded, "Easy peasy. I could print them at Kinko's for free," I said. "We don't have to decide now. All of us should have good photos anyway. We'll ask Ron to do it."

Giselle nodded, excitement tickling her face. Billie was chewing on a lock of hair, not saying anything. Giselle poked her and she nodded her agreement to get new photos.

"Where would we go?" I asked. "Wolfgang says there's a pretty good wrestling scene in Tampa. That'd be going home for me."

"The Grahams run that territory," Billie said. "They don't usually have too many women on their cards but it wouldn't hurt to try."

Giselle said, "My family owns a condo right outside of Miami. We might be able to stay there until we figure things out."

"Miami, ahhhh," Billie said, a dreamy look softening her features. "Pina coladas, beaches, tanned skin. Sounds good."

"We should probably wait to tell Brandy," I said. "I'll see if I can get the photoshoot lined up and we can tell her then. That'll be less time she'll have to keep a secret."

I thrust out my hand, palm down, in the center of our group and looked at them. Giselle slapped her hand on top of mine and Billie hesitated and then topped us off. "One, two, three. Go team!" We dreamed about a Moolah-less future in Miami.

After a while, I started getting anxious about the article.

"I'm going to have to kick you guys out," I said. "I promised my mom a letter." Giselle hugged me and they both headed back to her house, their heads close together.

They were halfway down the lake road when I opened my reporter's notebook. I flipped to the Black cop's number. He picked up on the second ring. I reintroduced myself and told him that I was freelancing for the Black News.

"Whoah. Did you say the Black News?" he asked. "I bet you didn't tell those Klan goons about that. You got some balls on you, girl."

"Ovaries," I said. "I've got solid steel ovaries. Much stronger than balls." I double-checked that he was still willing to let me interview him.

"It was risky to have you work the rally," I said. "Did you volunteer or were you assigned?" He took a breath and let it out slowly.

"It was all hands on deck, but I would've volunteered anyway," he said. "In the briefing, they told us that we were there to keep the peace and protect the Klan's First Amendment right to free speech."

"I'm sure that's true," I said.

"That rally was a powder keg. But, to tell you the truth, I was more worried about what would happen afterward. We patrolled the roads for a couple of hours after the rally. We wanted to make sure that none of them bubbas went out looking for Black people to hurt. The Black News, hunh? You were lucky they didn't find out who you're writing for."

"I told them I was on freelance assignment, which is true," I said, biting down on the plastic cap of my pen.

I started with some easy questions like where he was from (Columbia boy, born and bred), how long he'd been with the police (seven years after a stint in the army) and whether he liked his job (it's the only thing he ever wanted to do). Then it was down to what I really wanted to know, something readers could connect with.

"So, what was it like for you to be at that rally, hearing all those horrible things they were saying?" He took so long to reply, I thought he might've hung up.

"Well, first of all, don't call it a rally. That makes it sound fun like NASCAR," he said. "I have two opinions, one is me as an officer of the law, and the other is me as a Black man living in the South."

I took notes in my own brand of shorthand, racing to keep up with him.

"As a police officer, it's my job to uphold the Constitution," he said. "I was there to defend the Klan's right to free speech. As a Black man, I hate that a racist group like the KKK still exists in the United States. I pity the poor White people who join this group, looking for someone to blame for all the bad things in their lives. They cluster together because it makes them feel brave, but they're really full of hate and fear."

I still hadn't gotten to the emotional part of the question so I pressed him.

"How I felt? I was keyed up because we didn't know how many people would show. It wasn't so many in the end. It couldn't have been more than about 100 people. Good thing they didn't advertise free food. There would've been a lot more. Moving it away from town was smart. But they could've brought guns, so we had to be on our toes. I'm relieved it's over and no one got hurt. We did our jobs. How's that?"

By the time we finished talking, he'd convinced me that the North Carolina group wasn't going to find new members in South Carolina. With the last interview done, I concentrated on finishing a rough draft before second practice.

I started to worry about adding my name to the article. Fear spiked through me and I remembered the mantra from the movie "Dune." "Fear is a mind-killer. ...I will face my fear. I will permit it to pass over me and through me. ..." I repeated it until I felt calmer and kept working.

Chapter 27

KLAN BYLINE

After Thursday's second practice, I read through my article again, correcting typos and smoothing out transitions. I tucked the notebook in my backpack and drove to the Black News. It was after hours, but the receptionist was still at her desk and waved me in. Tyrell and his staff stood up when I entered.

Eight-by-ten photos littered the table. Beaming, the staff photographer pulled out a chair near her and we went through the images. There was pot-bellied Walter shoveling pork into his pie-hole. In the background, the officer I'd interviewed stood as still and grim as an Easter Island statue. Another photo focused tightly on Glenn Miller's crazy eyes and twisted mouth, spittle shooting toward the audience. He was blurred in the background of another, the focus on a man tying the rag around the cross. Then there was a series of images of the cross burning, from unlit to full blaze, the Klan and its supporters forming a semi-circle 20 feet away.

"If your story is half as good as these photos, we have a winner," Tyrell said. I needed the freelance money, but his praise meant a lot to me too. I'd delivered on my promise. He reached out and shook my hand and, without thinking, pulled me in for a hug. Two beats later, I excused myself to go type my article into a nearby computer.

I was getting ready to save the story to a floppy disc when I considered again whether to include my byline. If I added my name, would the Klan jerks come after me? Would they burn a cross on my front lawn? Would Moolah find out about the article and send me packing? But if I didn't put my name on it, I couldn't claim the article and photos.

"Fuck it," I thought, adding my byline and taking the disc to the editor. I used my real name, not Pippi or Stretch or Mad Maxine, and headed back to camp.

On the drive back, I started second-guessing myself. I wasn't in the phonebook yet but my number and address were available through the 411 operator. The next morning, I called the phone company to see if I could get my number removed from their directory. But the operator informed me it'd take at least a week to make the change. I couldn't believe I hadn't thought of it in time.

They published the story on Friday morning and by evening the phone calls had started.

"You're going to be sorry you wrote that story, bitch," a deep male voice drawled on the end of the line. "We're going to burn your house down with you in it."

I set the phone down softly and put the answering machine on. I changed the message to, "No one is home right now, please leave a message." I stopped answering all together.

By Saturday, I turned the ringer off. It made a clicking noise when anyone left a message. I'd hear that click and my muscles would tense. Most of the callers were men with thick southern accents, which somehow made what they were saying even more menacing. Several of the callers spoke in high wheedling tenors. I imagined shrewish men with ropy arms on the end of the line. After the answering machine had reached its limit, I went through the messages. I'd listen to a single syllable, which is all it took to detect the venom and hit erase. I didn't want to miss calls from Connie or Keith.

Chapter 28

STUDIO PORTRAITS

I slept fitfully but didn't want to reschedule our photoshoot with Ron. Not only was he willing to do individual portraits, he even suggested group shots. Late Sunday morning, I took the backroad out of the compound. I made sure no one saw me since old-timers were the only ones who were officially allowed to use the back exit. Giselle, Billie, and Brandy left through the main gate half an hour later, so we weren't seen leaving together.

Ron's studio was on the top floor of a dilapidated 1930s tourist home. The still-graceful building had been taken over by artists attracted to the low rent and buckets of light splashing through floor-to-ceiling windows. I parked in the shade of an old oak not far from an empty swimming pool.

I stomped up the steps, duffel slung over my shoulder. It was jammed with accessories and costume parts scrounged from thrift stores. Under one arm, I carried the box containing my precious new boots and a couple of leather and silver studded wrist cuffs I'd bought at the Harley Davidson store. Without the money from the freelance article, I wouldn't have been able to afford any of it. I mentally thanked the Black News.

Ron pulled the door open as I hit the top step.

"Right on time." He smiled and reached for my bag. "I can manage my own bags," I said, walking past him into the giant open space.

Photos of women dominated an entire wall. I recognized some of Raquel's haircut shots, but there were also thin models on the catwalk and Rubenesque "dolls" lolling nude in a clear spring. Clearly, Ron liked women.

In one corner, he'd set up lights in front of a white paper backdrop.

"The others will be here soon," I said. "It'll give us a little time to figure out some poses for the group shot."

Ron was a terrific studio photographer, but I had some ideas too. Ron tilted his head to the side. Clearly, he hadn't figured on working with Ms. Bossy Boots.

"Can I get you something to drink?" he called from a kitchen framed within the loft. I followed him and grabbed a seat at a red enamel table, which looked original to the place. I accepted a glass of water.

"I had an idea that I wanted to run by you," I said, pulling out a library book. I opened the page I'd marked and showed him one of my favorite Rembrandt paintings. In The Night Watch, the artist moved the viewers' eyes across the militia to the captain, using diagonal spears. I also liked Rembrandt's use of a dark background with patches of light.

"I see what you mean," Ron said. "I like it. Actually, if it's not too on the nose, I have something like a spear that could create that same effect." He put down his drink and dug into a closet at the far end of the space. He replaced the white backdrop with a black one and set a tall stool in the center.

"Why don't we have you sit with one girl on either side of you and one in front, kneeling," he said. "Giselle should kneel.

Billie and, what was the other girl's name? Brandy, that's right. One of them will hold the spear."

"It should be Billie. She's the most experienced one in our group and I want her to stand out."

"Sure," he said. "Let's try it a bunch of different ways."

He scooted his chair so close I could feel the heat of his body.

"So, tell me about yourself," he said. "How'd a nice girl like you end up in wrestling school?"

I was tempted to tell him the real story but decided against it with my friends arriving so soon.

"I've always been good at sports and I love anything to do with costumes. Can I show you the costumes I brought and maybe get some feedback on what will work best?"

I was banking on the fact that he, like most men, love giving advice. I swung my bag onto the table and unzipped it.

He stood next to me. "You don't seem like someone who'd go into wrestling. You could do a million things. Why risk breaking your neck?"

"Why ride a motorcycle?" I parried. "One asshole has an extra shot of tequila and you're road pizza. Life is risky. Wrestling is a cool job."

"Fair point. It's just ... I'd hate to see you get hurt."

Keith edged his way into my thoughts. It had been a couple of days since I'd gotten the note about his family emergency. We hadn't actually talked about being exclusive, so I didn't think I was breaking any rules. I silently recited an Edna St. Vincent Millay poem I used to justify wanton sex.

What lips my lips have kissed, and where, and why,
I have forgotten, and what arms have lain
Under my head till morning; but the rain
Is full of ghosts tonight, that tap and sigh

Upon the glass and listen for reply,
And in my heart there stirs a quiet pain
For unremembered lads that not again
Will turn to me at midnight with a cry.

Suddenly, I didn't want Ron to be an unremembered lad. I grabbed his belt buckle and pulled him the last few inches toward me. He was a smidge taller. Hot energy zinged through my body. He was watching my lips as we moved into a kiss. Someone pounded on the door and we sprang apart. Brandy pushed in, not waiting for an answer.

"We're here," she sang out.

Giselle and Billie came up behind her. They'd been playing some kind of fanny tag because Giselle was swatting Billie's hand away, telling her to "stop it." Love or lust was in the air.

"Come in, come in." Ron gestured them to the kitchen table and pulled up chairs. After offering everyone cold drinks, he sketched out what we'd decided. Billie would hold a spear angling from Giselle to the top of my mohawk. Giselle would crouch in front of us. He explained how the direction of the spear would connect Billie, standing on the left and slightly behind me, to the whole group. He looked at me for approval and I nodded. He had totally gotten what I'd proposed.

"Plus, it'll make you look extra tough," I told Billie. "Time to get changed."

Ron pointed to a bathroom at the back of the space. "Plenty of room for everyone." He checked his watch. "I have another shoot this afternoon so if you can be ready in 20 minutes, that should leave just enough time to do the group shots and a set of portraits."

We staked out separate corners in the bathroom. I undressed

and slipped on my black unitard. My hair was drooping a little so I hit it with more hairspray.

"Brandy, do you think you could do my makeup again?" She was tugging on a sarong-like outfit made from a piece of flowered fabric. A fuchsia hibiscus flower behind her ear and raffia anklets and, voila, she would transform into a Polynesian princess.

"Sure, give me a second to do my own makeup and I'll be right there." I checked my watch. Only 10 minutes left.

Her hand was steady as she applied her own eyeliner but time was ticking by. "I'll go ahead and get started and maybe you can tidy it up," I said.

I called "five minutes" and we scrambled to finish. All except Billie, who had put on a bathing suit with reinforced elastic at the legs, brushed her hair and called it done. Giselle gelled her hair to make it extra curly and then slipped on a thin white crop top under a suspendered leotard. Billie wrestled the misting bottle from Giselle.

"That's my job," Billie said. By the time she was done spritzing, Giselle was properly perky. What the heck, I thought. Part of what we sell is sex appeal.

"We're ready," I said as we filed back into the loft space. Ron had his camera mounted on a tripod in front of a black paper backdrop. He grabbed his chest as if he was having a heart attack. "You look amazing."

He directed me to a stool and placed the others in the positions he had described. He brought Billie the spear and looked through the camera to study the results. He adjusted the box lamp to set highlights in our eyes and shifted an umbrella light to create haloes around our heads.

A rap on the door and a big black Doberman appeared at the end of a leash, followed by Raquel, our good friend and hair magician.

"I thought you might like Rufus to be in the pictures," she said, scratching the massive dog's head. "He looks like a tough son of a bitch but he's really a lovebug," she said. I leaned down to let the pooch sniff my hand. Instead, he looked into my face, wagged his stub of a tail, and licked my nose.

"Wow, what a sweetie. But will you be able to see him against the black backdrop?" I asked Ron.

"Sure, with the lights I have, you'll be able to see the outline of his body and the glint of his eyes," Ron said. "You hold his leash, Pippi."

Raquel pulled a chair over and sat behind Ron. When he'd gotten us all into position, she popped in to tidy our hair and zap us with hairspray. These two had adopted us and that was okay with me.

Ron took a bunch of shots with and without the spear and then rearranged us. He put Billie on the stool with Giselle and me at her shoulder and Brandy crouched in front.

He moved onto individual shots, which was really fun. Not surprisingly, he loved Giselle's wet T-shirt, begging to be the one to re-wet it

We'd been posing for an hour and a half, when Ron glanced at his watch and said we'd have to wind things up.

"I'll get a contact sheet to you in a week or so." He unscrewed the camera from the tripod and began packing it away. "I won't have time to make prints but I have a friend who will do it for you fast and cheap."

He said good-bye, lingering a little longer when he hugged me. "Give me a call. I'd like to finish our discussion." I pressed my cheek to his.

We all walked down the stairs together. Once we were outside the building, the girls started ribbing me. "So, you and Ron, hunh?" Brandy said.

"I thought you and Keith were together," Giselle said. "Not that I'm being judgmental, but I didn't figure you for a slut." She smiled and wrapped her arm around Billie's waist.

"It's kind of hard for me to pass that up," I admitted. Brandy nodded her head, grinning.

"You know what I mean," I said.

"Yep, I would definitely fuck him," she said. I was pretty sure Brandy wasn't a virgin, but I winced hearing a 16-year-old talk like this.

"That's one big thing done," I said. "First the pictures, then the brochure. We'll be ready if we decide to make a move."

Chapter 29

RED PICKUP

Monday morning arrived like a rude and unwelcome guest. After an espresso, I dragged myself to the ring and willed myself to get through it. The burned-out feeling disappeared after the first bump. My spine cracked as though I was getting a chiropractic adjustment and I relaxed into the workout. The slaps and punches didn't even hurt as much. Before I knew it, two hours had zipped by and it was time to get showered and ready for work. I tied a red bandana over my mohawk so I didn't spook the customers.

Things got weird the minute I left Camp Moolah. Idling outside the gate was a red pickup with a confederate flag decal on the back window. My internal alarm started clanging. I sunk down in my seat and drove to the end of the block, but the creep had seen me. He made a U-turn and pulled up fast behind me. He stayed inches from my bumper the whole way downtown. Was he one of those assholes who'd left me a phone message?

I glanced back through the rearview mirror. The driver met my eyes and mouthed something mean. I stuck to the speed limit and prayed for a traffic cop to pull this joker over for tailgating. No such luck.

I imagined what Pippi Longstocking would do. She'd find a way to outfox her opponent. The "strongest girl in the world" would pick up the truck, twirl it on the point of her index finger and toss it in a picturesque Swedish pond. The racist goober would emerge covered in duckweed.

Back in the real world, I beelined straight to the police station, which I'd taken the precaution of locating when the horrible calls had started. I pulled into the parking lot. The pickup driver peeling off with a long blast of his car horn that played the first few notes of Dixie. I had a death grip on the steering wheel as I parked near the front door.

I sat and took deep breaths to calm myself and headed to the station. Behind the heavy glass door, an ancient officer with an accent as thick as his neck looked up from a gray tanker desk.

"What can I do for you, little lady?" I blanched inwardly at the careless sexism, but held my peace. I asked for Officer Earle, the Black cop, and he pointed me to some battered plastic chairs. While I waited, I flipped through a tattered copy of Field and Stream and read a tongue in cheek article about the forgetfulness of deer hunters. I was about to learn about the ethics of high-tech fishing, when my cop walked through the front door.

"Someone to see you, bubba," thick-neck drawled, nodding to where I sat. The tall, built cop looked over, recognition dawning. He came over with his hand extended.

"Do you have a minute? I need to talk to you." I looked over his shoulder through the door and saw the red pickup pass by.

"Quick, look out the door. That's the guy who followed me here." The officer turned around but my tailgater had already driven off.

"Why don't you come to my desk and we can talk," he said.

The old cop made a big show of shoving himself up from the desk, lumbering to the front door and spitting out a big loogie. Did he object to me meeting with his fellow officer? I put him out of my mind. We walked to a desk with a scenic view of the parking lot.

"We enjoyed your article. You did a real fine job," he said. "Great pictures too. You really nailed that messed-up scene."

"Thanks. But the article's the problem," I said. "Those assholes from North Carolina said they'd get me if they didn't like what I wrote. Now, I'm getting all these phone calls, which wasn't that big a deal until today. Someone was waiting for me outside the camp and tailgated me all the way here."

"I can fill out the paperwork later," he said. "Tell me exactly what happened."

I described verbatim the kind of things they were saying on the phone. He frowned but asked me to continue.

"At first, I let it roll off my back. Sticks and stones, you know," I said. "They have my address now and I'm scared. I bet the driver is part of the Klan. Here's his tag number."

I handed him a piece of paper. It hadn't been easy to read the license plate numbers in the rearview but I'd managed. He asked me where I lived. I paused and explained about Camp Moolah.

"There's the main gate that almost everyone uses and a back entrance that's kind of hidden away. And there's a high fence around the property. Plus, there are watchdogs. So, that's good. The thing is, no one there knows that I wrote the article. They can't find out I'm a journalist. They'd kick me out."

"So, we need to find a way to protect you without letting your wrestling buddies know what's going on? That's going to be tough." He paused and thought for a minute. "I guess I can find out who the truck belongs to and go have a chat with them. I can probably get a car to swing by the camp to check whether he's hanging around. They'll radio us if something's going on. But I can't post anyone full time unless they come after you. And it doesn't sound like you'd really want that anyway."

"Come after me?" I said in a panic. "You mean, attack me?" I sat back in my chair.

"That's about the size of it," he said. "Is there anywhere else you can stay for the next few days?" I thought about Keith, but his place was all the way downtown and I didn't want to bring him into this mess. On the other hand, he might be my only real option.

"I'm seeing a guy. I can ask him. But I still have to get in and out of the compound for training." I thought it over. "I guess I could take the back way and hope they don't find it on their own."

"Stay somewhere else, at least for now. I'll send out a patrol a couple of times a day. We'll adjust our plan from there." We stood and he gave me a firm handshake.

"What about the officer at the front?" I said. "He didn't seem to like you talking to me. Any chance he's in the Klan?"

"Nah, I don't think so," he said. "He's old, and jealous that a beautiful woman like you asked for me."

Beautiful woman? I'd been so focused on making my report that his comment caught me by surprise. Officer Earle flashed a dazzling smile and gave me that look. I'm a sucker for muscular arms and his were huge and well proportioned. His pheromones washed over me like a summer shower. I felt that familiar tingle and was tempted. But I flash-forwarded to the scene where he found my stash of pot and had to decide whether to throw me in the pokey. I talked myself out of it.

"I've got to get to work," I said, giving him a friendly smile. I wish I could hire you as my bodyguard. Can I call you if things get weird?" He nodded and held the door open for me. He walked me to my car, scanning the road in case the hillbilly was nearby.

"Take care of yourself," I called out my window. "Same to you," he said.

I don't remember driving to Kinko's or my shift. I was on autopilot, helping customers, making copies. My mind was chewing on what I might face when I returned home. I had finished copying someone's dissertation, when Dave appeared at my elbow.

"Are you okay, Pippi?"

I explained about the red pickup. Alarm spread over his face.

"You have got to be careful with those people. They've done some really bad things," he said. "A few years ago, Miller's group went after a Black prison guard just because he had applied for a supervisor's position. The Klan pulled out all the stops to keep him from getting the job."

Dave opened up a box of paper and we started restocking.

"First, they burned a cross on his front lawn, then they scratched KKK on his daddy's pickup. Things got really bad. Another prison guard showed up at his house and threatened him with a 22."

"Did the Black guard get shot?"

"I don't remember," Dave said. "Does it matter?"

I told Dave about enlisting the help of Officer Earle and, though he was not a fan of police in general, he thought this was a good move.

"Let me know if you need any help, okay? I'd never forgive myself if anything happened to you."

I reached out and hugged him. Dave was a good friend

when I needed one. We finished stacking paper, sweeping the floor, and replacing ink cartridges.

"Yikes! I've got to get going or I'll be late to practice." I looked out the door for the red pickup but I didn't see it. They hadn't figured out where I worked at least.

Chapter 30

SOARING SUPLEX

I drove past the compound to see if anyone was stalking me outside the gate. No one there, thank god. I went around the block and double-checked again. As an extra precaution, I took the back road and parked behind my house. I didn't want him spying my car in case that rat bastard snuck onto the property far enough to see my car. I slipped into my house in time to change and made it to practice with my normal group.

I was glad to be back in the training ring, not worried about the Klan freaks. The door to the training room was closed, which meant I was late again. Linda and Zoey were in the ring surrounded by the girls. I rolled into the ring, grateful that they ignored me. I tried to catch Giselle's eye while Linda explained the move, but she didn't look over.

"There are a lot of different suplexes," Linda said. "This one's called the soaring suplex." She gestured to Zoey to her side.

"It starts with putting a front face lock on your opponent," she said. "You remember the front face lock, right?"

Linda reached out and grabbed Zoey's hair and, quick as you please, tucked her head into her right elbow with her butt sticking away from her. Linda then slung Zoey's right arm around her neck.

"The next thing you're going to do is lift her straight above you," Linda explained. "There's no way in hell you can muscle her up all by yourself. So you've got to give your partner a signal that you're going up. That way, she knows when to kick off the ground and throw her legs up in the air."

In the perfect suplex, the woman on the ground has a medium wide stance before kicking up, she explained. The two wrestlers connect at the shoulder and the airborne woman points her toes to the sky. The move ends in a double back bump, she said.

"You can walk around the ring, build up some tension, before falling back onto the mat."

Linda paired me with Zoey. She was hard to hoist, but we finally got a rhythm going. I suplexed her and then, reluctantly, she suplexed me. She was probably remembering the disastrous flying head scissors, but there were no mishaps this time. I would definitely use this move when I finally got some matches, I decided. It was dramatic as hell and didn't hurt.

We repeated the move and then worked on combinations until practice was over. Giselle headed out the door without waiting for me. I caught up with her at the end of the driveway.

"Hey, wait up." She slowed but didn't turn around. When I caught up with her, she looked pissed off. I guessed she'd been hiding it during training, but out here she didn't bother.

"What's going on? When are you going to start practicing with the old faces?" She shook her head and lunged at a clutch of ducks, scattering them on the road.

"Seriously, Giselle. What happened?" She still didn't speak. Instead, she nodded me in the direction of her house.

She threw open her front door and ran to the couch. She

grabbed a cushion and screamed into it. What the hell? I grabbed her shoulders and turned her toward me.

"What's wrong? Tell me!" Her face crumpled and she looked like a little girl. I led her over to the kitchen table and got her a glass of water.

"Take your time," I said. "Breathe. Whatever it is, we'll figure it out." She sipped the water. After a while, she calmed down.

"Before practice, Linda told me that Moolah changed her mind," she said. "She's not going to book me like she said she would. She said that things were messed up when green girls thought they called the shots." Giselle took another sip.

"That's bullshit, Giselle. Why is she sitting on your career? It doesn't make sense."

"Moolah says she can only introduce one girl at a time and she's chosen you," Giselle said. "She said it'll be months before she'll bring anyone else to Poughkeepsie."

I knew that Poughkeepsie was where WWF taped its TV matches.

"She also said that other girls who've been here longer should come first ... like Wanda."

"Wanda? Are you fucking kidding me?" I blurted out. "Moolah's messing with you. This was more of the divide and conquer bullshit she was doing with Billie and me."

The evil queen was manipulating us and I was sick of it.

"We've got to get out of here. Soon."

Giselle turned a blotchy face to me. "Do you think we really can?"

"I do. Let's tell Billie and Brandy what happened. Until then, act normal. Don't worry. It's going to be great."

Later that night, the four of us met at Giselle's house. Before we arrived, Giselle spoke with her parents who agreed to let us borrow their condo in Miami. We had a place to stay. We just had to get there.

Giselle and I both had cars. Hers was tiny but she didn't have much stuff. Neither did Brandy. Billie, on the other hand, had mementos from her half dozen years of wrestling—costumes, wrestling boots, photo albums, and all the normal household stuff too. My car was roomy but I'd have to pare down my belongings to make room for Billie's stuff.

"Since we'll be living together, we only need one of everything," I said. "All of us have kitchen stuff so let's take the best and leave the rest behind." We made a list of all the things we needed to bring with us.

"I can probably fit all of your stuff, Billie. You and Giselle can drive together and Brandy can ride with me. Then we can trade off. We should caravan together in case one of us breaks down." I went to the kitchen for a glass of water.

"We'll need gas money to get there and some start-up cash until we start getting bookings," Billie said. "Moolah hasn't been booking me lately so I don't have much saved. But you can have it all."

"I've saved some money from my job and have a little left from a check my mom sent," I volunteered. I had felt uneasy cashing my mom's $500 check, but car insurance and telephone bills had forced the issue. An achy feeling of love rose in my chest. My mom was keeping me afloat even though she disapproved of my choice.

"I've got about $200 saved up," Giselle said. "But we're going to be staying for free at my parents' condo, so maybe someone else can cover the gas."

Brandy bit her lip. "All I have is $50 and that's got to last me for the month," she said.

"Don't worry about it," I said. "We'll be okay. If we leave soon, we won't have to pay next month's rent."

A little spark of excitement kindled inside me. We were going to show Moolah she couldn't kick us around anymore. Or pimp us out. Or take our money. She was going to regret being such a flaming asshole.

Chapter 31

FIREMAN'S CARRY

I was up before the sun to tackle my to-do list. Over cafe con leche, I reviewed my tasks. I would write bios for the promotional brochure, find out when the contact sheets would be ready and how soon I could get prints made. I'd also check in with Keith about his family emergency and Officer Earle to see if they had netted any Klanners in my neighborhood.

Last but not least, I needed to get my head straight for the next evening's practice with the veterans. I didn't want a repeat of my first practice when Moolah had dragged me around like a rag doll. I needed to be on my game.

When I got to the ring, Giselle was whispering to Brandy. Linda put her hands on her hips and stared at them until they stopped.

"Today, you're learning the fireman's carry and airplane spin," Linda said.

In the fireman's carry, you grab your opponent's right wrist and pull her arm up and over your shoulders, she said. As you pull her onto your shoulder, you squat and hook your other arm through her legs.

"You stand up with the girl across your shoulders and that's the fireman's carry," she said. "To do the airplane spin, you start spinning as fast as you can. When you stop, you can either drop her in front or behind you. This isn't a hard move but it's like the suplex. You've got to work together. If you're the one who's getting spun, you need to jump up when she gives you the signal. Don't make her muscle you up," Linda said.

I worked with Wanda but she couldn't get the timing right. She always leaped before I'd started to stand. In the end, I just grabbed her and hoisted her up using new muscles that had popped out in the last few months.

I was nervous, thinking about that guy in the red pickup. Was he going to come after me? Would Moolah notice and send someone out there to ask him what the hell he was doing? A jog after practice would help calm me but running around the lake was out of the question. I decided to drive to Keith's place and jog in his neighborhood. I packed two sets of clothes: one for work and the second for the afternoon practice.

I held my breath as I pulled into the neighborhood from the back road but the red pickup wasn't outside the gate. I made it to the highway undetected and headed downtown. I hadn't heard from Keith since his note and wasn't expecting to see him. But there he was, throwing a suitcase in the back of his 280Z. He shut the hatch and looked up. His hair was mussed, his face pale and haggard. Dark circles ringed his eyes.

"I'm so glad you're here," I said, walking over and giving him a hug. He was stiff at first, like he'd forgotten that we were lovers. But I held on and, after a few seconds, he melted into me.

"My dad had a heart attack," he said. "It's bad. He's in the ICU. Mom's by herself. I have to get back as soon as I can." He opened up the car door.

"Oh, Keith. I'm so sorry," I said. "I wish I could come with you but Moolah booked my first match and I can't miss practice." I made myself stop talking. His father's health was so much more important than some stupid match.

"I'm happy for you, Pippi," he said. "But I've got to go."

He opened the car door and paused, torn between the need to hit the road and the need for comfort. I pulled him into my arms again and gave him a bear hug.

"What hospital is he in? I'll come as soon as I can," I said into his soft blond hair.

"He's at the Abbeville County Hospital, about 100 miles away. Here, I'll give you directions." He started to reach for his bag for a pen but I stopped him.

"That's okay. I have a map. Go on, now. Take care of your mom."

I hadn't had a chance to tell him about the article or the Klan rednecks chasing me or about my plans to leave Columbia. I felt bad. I hadn't intended to, but I was probably going to break his heart a little.

"Before you go," I said through the car window. "Is it okay if I stay at your place for a few days? I need to get out of Crazyland."

Distracted, he nodded.

I made him promise to call with an update. I waved goodbye, a yellow ball of dread forming in my stomach. Go for a run, I ordered myself.

I jogged to the university running track, about a mile away. I started with a bunch of wind sprints down the green middle. It was too easy to get winded in the ring. Good lungs would get me through my matches.

A bunch of jocks loped around the outside lanes. They kept glancing my way, but I ignored them. I didn't time to spare for their nonsense. I stopped when I'd sweated through my jersey and then slowly jogged back to Keith's.

During the run, I had mentally written bios for the brochure and made notes when I got back to his house. I described myself as a genetic experiment gone awry and Billie as a veteran powerhouse who'd battled wrestling greats in the squared circle. Giselle was a high-speed grappler whose beauty masked an evil heart and Brandy was a Polynesian princess schooled in ancient wrestling techniques.

After an hour or so, I put the bios aside and called Ron. His answering machine kicked on but I thought he might be screening calls.

"Hi, Ron. Pick up, pick up, pick up." I paused for a second. "It's Pippi. My situation at Camp Moolah has gotten sticky. I'm calling to see if you might be able to speed things up with the contact sheets. I'm staying at a friend's so you can call me here." I left him Keith's number.

After a pounding shower, I wrapped myself in Keith's robe and scrambled some eggs with salsa and jalapeños.

I rinsed out my workout clothes and hung them on the porch to dry. I pictured my younger self handing clothespins to my mom while she hung up our clothes. A wave of tenderness rolled over me. I still had a little time left before practice so I decided to write her a letter.

Dear Mom,

I know it's been a long time between letters. Sorry about that. So much is going on. I'm finally catching onto the wrestling thing though it was really hard. First, they teach you a whole bunch of moves and make you do them a million times until you can do them automatically. I guess it makes sense when you think about it. I recently graduated to working out with the veteran lady wrestlers and I'll have my first match soon. I'm learning a lot more of the inside stuff, all the theatrics that go along with wrestling. (You know how I love drama!) Before you start to worry, I haven't been injured. I'm fine. And I've been able to keep my hand in journalism. I did a freelance article for a paper called the Black News, so at least I'll have that to put on my resume when I go back to the real world. I love and hate South Carolina. People are friendly but they still fly the confederate flag on the capitol building if you can believe that.

Thanks for the check and your letter. The cash came at the perfect time. I'll use some of it to get down to Miami where one of my wrestling buddies has a family condo. A group of us are leaving Moolah, a really horrible person, and starting our own group. Lots to do between now and when we leave. Wish me luck! I'll call you when we get settled.

Love you tons, Pippi

There was so much I didn't say. I couldn't mention that Moolah was a pimp and a thief or that she had a network of spies delivering information to her.

On the way home, I stopped at a grocery to restock my larder. I bought cans of garbanzos to make my favorite curry. I also stocked up on crackers, peanut butter, and sardines, foods that wouldn't go bad if we hit the road sooner rather than later.

I took the dirt road to the back entrance. Right before I disappeared behind a tree, I snuck a glance at the main entrance on Moolah Drive. Sure enough, a red truck idled outside the gate, cigarette smoke curling from the driver's window. I wanted him gone. Moolah couldn't find out about the article I'd written.

After stowing the food, I walked the long way around the lake to the training ring so the stalker couldn't see me. Giselle and Brandy were standing in front of the building, waiting for me. I walked straight in. Loitering outside would make me a target, given that the training ring stood 50 yards from the gate where the idiot idled.

Linda sat in a lawn chair near the ring, which put her at eye level with Darlene. They were deep in a whispered conference. Linda's frown lines gouged deeper than usual and Darlene seemed agitated.

When I walked by, Darlene whispered, "Kayfabe," code for "shut up, there's a mark around." I guess they considered me a clueless rube. They resumed whispering after I passed. It was obvious that they didn't want me to overhear their conversation.

I slid onto the apron and into the ring. I started hitting the ropes. I ran across and threw myself into the ropes, sprang off, and ran across to the other side and hit them again. I knew I'd have striped bruises tomorrow but I kept running back and forth, over and over. I ran the crisscross patterns, all the while wondering about Linda and Darlene's secret.

Chapter 32

20 MOVES OF DOOM

I had swabbed the ring and brought Linda coffee for two weeks, the price for missing a practice to cover the Klan rally. My obligation was fulfilled, but I kept bringing Linda coffee to keep her sweet.

Wednesday morning, I tapped on her door and handed her the java. She passed me the empty cup from the previous day. I was turning away when she told me to wait. She went back inside and returned with a piece of notebook paper.

"These are the moves you'll be doing in your first match," she croaked. "Memorize them. You'll run through them with Moolah and me tonight. You can skip the regular afternoon practice."

I wanted to say that my match wasn't for ages and why did I need this list now? But Linda seemed to read my mind.

"You're flying up to New York on Friday morning. Your first match is Saturday and you'll spend two nights up there. Pack light. Just your wrestling gear and one change of clothes"

My mouth fell open. I thought I would have a lot more time before my first match. My pals and I had plans to weed through our stuff and pack this weekend. Holy crap.

The phone was ringing when I got home. I left the answering

machine on in case it was the Klan asshole but I picked up when I heard Ron's voice.

"I had some extra time so I went ahead and printed out copies of the pictures," he said. "I was hoping I could see you when you stop by to pick them up."

His voice rumbled like a motorcycle revving up and I felt an answering tingle in my nether regions. I knew what he had in mind. I wouldn't have minded getting together but the timing was bad.

"I'd really like to see you but I just found out that my first match is this weekend. We leave for New York day after tomorrow and I have a ton of stuff to do before then. Would it be okay if Giselle picked up the photos later today?"

He sighed but agreed to leave a manila envelope for her inside his stairwell. After he hung up, I set my mind to memorizing the 20 moves on the list. They were all things I'd practiced a million times but the idea of doing them in front of an audience with an opponent was nerve-wracking. I broke them into five chunks and worked on them until heading to the practice ring.

I expected all of the veterans but it was just Linda, Moolah, and me.

"Before we do the moves, could we walk through where they'll happen in the ring?" I asked. She looked at me and shook her head like I was an idiot, but went through it anyway. It helped to know what move was happening where.

I thought I had them all memorized but the stress of being in the ring with Linda and Moolah scared them out of my head. At first, I could only remember two or three moves in a row before I had to ask for help.

We walked through it again and, this time, I remembered five moves in a row and then six. We were two hours into practice when I was finally able to remember all 20 moves. But doing the moves in the quiet of a training ring would be a lot different than doing them in front of screaming wrestling fans.

"Remember, you're not just doing the moves. You're selling what you and your partner are doing," Linda said. My face must've shown my panic because she patted my shoulder.

"You're just nervous. Don't worry. Moolah will be there with you. She'll help you."

Oh, yeah. Warm fuzzy Moolah. I'd gotten so used to Linda's billy goat gruffness, I didn't trust when she was nice.

"I'm trying. I can do this," I said. She smiled and nodded.

After dinner, I packed some more boxes. I stowed them in the back of my closet in case I had uninvited guests while I was away. I was almost finished packing, when I called it quits at midnight. I went to bed, sleeping in fitful, two- and three-hour chunks.

Chapter 33

GORILLA MONSOON

In my dream, I'd forgotten all the moves and was standing there like a lump in the middle of the ring. The alarm went off and I sat up like I'd been electrocuted. I was heading up to New York for my first match. Fuuuuck.

Even though it was pretty warm for February, I knew it would be chilly up north so I grabbed my heaviest coat. I walked over to Moolah's house and stowed my bag in the Cadillac's vast trunk. Linda waved Moolah and me off as we pulled out of the driveway. Darlene scowled in my general direction.

Our early flight to LaGuardia was uneventful and, after we landed, we made our way to the rental car desk. Moolah requested the biggest sedan they had and insisted on driving to WWF corporate headquarters, an hour away in Stamford, Connecticut. She pulled the bench seat all the way forward, so I had to cross my legs hard to the side to fit.

"When we get into the meeting, you let me do the talking," she said. She jammed a stick of gum into her mouth, but didn't offer me one.

We'd have a brief meeting with Vince Junior, she said. Thanks to Billie, I knew she meant Vince McMahon, Jr., owner of the WWF, and son of Vince McMahon, Sr. Moolah had had an exclusive contract with the father for years before he handed over the company – and the contract—to his son.

"Vince Junior and me are tight," she said. "That's why my girls do so good." That was a matter of opinion, I thought. Judging from the down-at-the heel lives of the women at the compound, it didn't look like anyone but Moolah was making money.

She drove like a bat out of hell, pressing her pedal to the metal the whole way. She passed within inches of a car on the left and overcorrected, leaving me lurching for the door handle. Forty minutes later, she pulled into the parking lot of a glitzy office building, narrowly missing a jogger.

A slender young woman in a tailored suit met us in the white leather and chrome reception area. The glitz disappeared when we stepped behind a set of double doors marked "Private."

She guided us through a maze of poorly lit corridors. Light streamed from an open door halfway down the hall. I heard the grunts before I saw the huge man in tiny shorts balancing a cartoonishly large barbell on his shoulders. Behind him, another muscle-bound brute bench-pressed 350 pounds without breaking a sweat. I couldn't tear myself away and had to jog to catch up with Moolah.

Past the muscle factory was a conference room dominated by a long polished table. At its head sat Gorilla Monsoon, Vince Junior's booker. He was making notes on a legal pad and didn't look up when we came in. We waited for an invitation to sit. Moolah, for all her long history with the company, was still waiting for permission.

I could tell he was tall, even sitting down. He may have been athletic at some point, but his belly now hung down below his belt. He looked like a cross between Diego Rivera, the mural painter, and Al Capone, the gangster. An unlit stogie stuck out the side of his mouth.

Moolah made small talk with Gorilla while beefcake paraded outside. I'd positioned myself so I could enjoy the view, but I planned to keep my hands off the wrestlers. I wasn't going to be an arena rat, the name they called the girls who slept with the wrestlers after the matches. I turned my attention back to the conversation when Moolah began talking about working me into an angle with Wendi Richter.

"I could bring her out as my secret weapon," said Moolah. She sat on the edge of her chair, ramrod straight. "I know she's got a kind of crazy look but I think it'd work well against Wendi." She paused and looked over at me.

"We might even let her win the belt." She winked at me. This was the cheese that she'd dangled in front of both Billie and me. I knew better than to believe her.

Gorilla nodded his head a fraction. "Might be." He pushed a stapled stack of papers toward me.

"I don't want to talk about strategy until we have a contract with your girl," he said. "Won't mean anything."

Uh oh. I hadn't realized they'd be asking me to sign legal papers today. I wasn't an idiot. I knew enough not to sign a contract without having a lawyer look at it. I told them as much, trying to be as gentle and unsuspicious sounding as possible.

"Go ahead and sign them, sugar," Moolah urged. "I promise you'll be happy you did." I saw that avaricious gleam and felt the power of her personality pushing me. I dug my heels in. There's nothing I hate worse than being pushed.

"I promise I'll have a lawyer look it over when we get back to Columbia and send it back to you first thing," I said.

Gorilla glowered at Moolah. I could read his thoughts, "You

can't keep control of your girls. Not good." Except I wasn't her girl, I was my own woman and had been since I was 10. I kept my face neutral and guileless.

She was chilly toward me on the drive to the civic center in Poughkeepsie where WWF taped its weekly show. I looked out at the skeletal trees on the barren winter scape and warmed myself with thoughts of moving to Miami. I smiled slightly, thinking about the moment she discovered that we'd left her behind.

She started regaining her good humor the nearer we got to the arena. "You do a good show today and fans will buy tickets to come see you out in the towns. If things work out, you'll be working seven days a week. Big fat paychecks, darling!"

I glanced at the hanging bag in the back seat. In it was Moolah's new purple sequined outfit. Everything seemed to be moving in slow motion. A few more turns and we were at the civic center. It was starting to hit me. Doing endless repetitions of moves in the training ring back in South Carolina was completely different from what I was now facing. She gave me a pep talk about the upcoming match.

"You listen to me, do exactly what I say, and you'll be fine. It'll be over before you know it."

We drove past a security guard and parked under the arena. My match was scheduled for 1:30 and it was only noon so I had plenty of time to get dressed. A smiling bouncer type in a black T-shirt opened her car door.

"It's nice to see you again, Moolah," he said. "Who'd you bring with you?" He peered past her to gawk at me. She slugged his shoulder.

"Good to see you too! Now you keep your hands off her, you old dog. We've got work to do." He grinned and took her bag.

She led the way to our dressing room, high heels tip-tapping down the long corridor. He unlocked a dressing room door and waved us in. In the glare of buzzing fluorescent lights were a full-length mirror, a sink, and a door leading to a small bathroom. My bladder was bursting so I excused myself. I sat there for a while, gathering my wits and courage. Moolah tapped on the door. "I need to get in there too, hon."

We traded places and while she was inside, I put on my black leotard suit, a wide copper belt, and my new motorcycle boots and leather cuffs. I perked up my mohawk with a ton of hairspray and embellished it with green and blue spray-on hair dye. Then I began to work on my eye makeup. She washed her hands and came over to where I was standing.

"Go heavy on the eyeliner and rouge," she instructed. "The lights wash you out so you need to put on more than you normally wear."

She followed her own advice and reapplied pancake foundation. She outlined her eyes like Cleopatra and drew in lips like an inept drag queen. I pulled out my acrylic paints and drew tribal patterns on my face and head.

I was starting to hyperventilate sitting in that little room, so I took a walk to the backstage area. Long curtains hung from the high ceilings, creating dark nooks. Inside one dim space, Hulk Hogan chatted up a wrestler in a Mexican luchador mask. In another nook, I recognized Wendi Richter by her wild mane of hair. She was standing by herself, looking through the curtain at the growing crowd. "Going to be a good house tonight," she said without turning. She was fit and pretty in her blue and red wrestling gear.

I was nervous but forced myself to say hello. "I wanted to introduce myself," I said. "I'm Mad Maxine. Moolah brought me."

Wendi gave me a cursory look, "hmphed", and walked away. I was bummed but figured Moolah probably had screwed her like she had all the other girls at camp. I was tainted by association.

I shook it off and made my way back to our dressing room. I watched two wrestlers acknowledge each other with the limpest of handshakes. It looked like a greeting you might get from an 80-year-old accountant right after he'd awakened from a long coma. It made sense in a way. A bunch of macho guys exchanging bone-crushing handshakes was bound to be a problem. Better to err on the side of gentleness.

"Max, get back here," Moolah called to me in the hallway. So now I wasn't Pippi or Stretch, I was Max. Okay by me, I thought. She was standing in the doorway fanning herself with a thick wad of cash.

"Put it in your boot," Moolah told me. "It's pay for you and the other girls who wrestled the last time I was here."

"You sure you want me to hold it?" It was at least a thousand bucks. I worried that it might somehow slip out during my match.

"I want you to feel what it's like to be rolling in dough. You stick with me, darling, and you're going to make a lot of money." I tucked the greenbacks in my boot and tightened the top strap.

We threaded our way back through the darkened hallways when we heard the starting bell for the second match. "Go get 'em," Hogan whispered behind me.

Chapter 34

FIRST MATCH

A security guard yanked the curtain aside and a wall of sound crashed down on my head. Moolah marched out in front of me, down a walkway lined by scary wrestling fans. They screamed for her blood. A woman in a giant Hawaiian muumuu waved a "Moolah sucks" sign right in the wrestler's face. Big mistake.

Moolah got right up close and screamed, "If I looked like you, I'd sue my parents and my grandparents." The woman gave as good as she got. "Why don't you retire from the ring, you old has-been? Nobody wants to see your saggy old ass in a bathing suit."

Instead of taking offense, Moolah put her hands on her hips and swaggered past her. I followed in her wake. I was astonished by the size of the arena, a veritable cathedral of pain. I plastered a scowl on my face and pumped my fist in the air.

I hopped on the apron of the ring, praying that people couldn't see my trembling legs. Moolah didn't get into the ring right away. She walked around it, pointing and yelling at the crowd and they yelled back. She began stabbing an accusatory finger at an old man in the front row.

"I've seen raisins with less wrinkles than you've got, old man," she said.

"Oh yeah? Why don't you look in the mirror, you old hag?" At some unseen signal, she walked up the steps into the ring. That made him even madder and he continued to curse her.

A tuxedoed announcer moved to the center of the ring. It was "Mean Gene" Okerlund, a former wrestler turned announcer. He reached for an old-fashioned mike that had been lowered from the ceiling. Moolah and I stomped around the ring while Gene introduced the wrestlers.

"First of all, to my right, from Oklahoma, weighing in at 140 pounds, Susan Starr." He dragged out her name so it was "Staaaaaaarr." My tiny but powerful adversary held both her arms up in a victory sign. The crowd cheered as she walked to each corner of the ring. She yanked off her black cowboy hat and white-fringed chaps until all she wore was a royal blue bathing suit and boots. I guessed they'd picked someone small to make me look extra big.

"Now, to introduce to you, the manager, the former ladies' champion, the Fabulous Moolaaaaah." The crowd simultaneously booed and screamed at the sound of her name. Then it was my turn.

"And ladies and gentlemen, at 6 feet four inches tall, Mad Maxinnnnnne."

I stomped around the ring, punching the air. I was glad I had on my punk sunglasses because the crowd couldn't see the whites of my eyes.

Moolah called me to our corner and I began handing her parts of my costume. My fingers were trembling as I unlaced the cuffs but I finally got them off. That left the belt and the choker. I began to walk away.

"Your glasses," Moolah hissed. I handed her my sunglasses

and moved to the center of the ring. The bell clanged and the match began.

Susan ducked under me as I lunged at her and fell into the ropes. I lunged for her again, a clumsy Frankenstein move, and again she ducked under my arms. The next time, I lunged into a turnbuckle, Susan was right behind me, taking me down and rolling me up in a tidy package. The ref was there for the three count but I kicked out of it.

On the sidelines, the ring commentators drove home the point. "Maxine is a little slow on the mark. Takedown by Susan Starr. Mad Maxine quickly kicking out. So far, Susan Starr is playing it smart. Keeping out of trouble."

At that point, I decided to take advantage of my superior strength. We went into a clench and I threw Susan to the ground twice in a row.

"That's what you get for locking up with Maxine," a commentator said. "She is so strong."

The third time I tried the same move, Susan outmaneuvered me and took me down with a drop toehold. I'd seen other girls do it but had never learned the move. She stuck out her feet and tripped me. I lurched forward like a felled Sequoia.

I was still on my stomach when she pulled one of my legs across the other and started working it. It didn't hurt but I was completely disabled. I sold it like she was breaking my leg, pounding the mat, and yelling.

From a seated position, she leaped into the air and pretended to slam down on my leg. I really couldn't get out of the hold so I reached back and tried to grab her hair. That didn't work so, as preordained, I worked my way over to my back and kicked her into the ropes. She pitched forward and I monkey flipped her onto her back.

"You get monkey flipped by someone like Maxine, it's like

getting body-slammed," the commentator said. "Those kinds of blows will have an effect on Starr." Susan was selling the move, making me look good.

I looked down at my boot and a hundred-dollar bill was sticking out. I leaned over and stuffed it back down.

I grabbed Susan around the neck. I pulled her up into a chokehold so that her face was even with mine. Susan grabbed me around my waist with her knees to reduce the pressure on her neck. I threw her down on her back. I walked around to yell at the crowd and came back to Susan who was still selling the move. I grabbed her by the hair and did it again. I was heaving, trying to catch my breath. We were getting close to the finish, a suplex. I desperately wanted the match to be over.

I put her in a front headlock, threw her arm over my neck, and pulled her up so her legs were sticking straight up in the air in a soaring suplex. I fell backward and then covered her body with mine until the ref smacked the mat for a three count. I rocked back on my haunches and raised my arms in victory. Moolah ducked under the ropes and ran over to me. She hoisted one of my hands in the air and the ref raised the other one.

Moolah dropped my hand and ran over to Susan who was still down on the mat. She gave her a few swift kicks in the ribs while the ref's back was turned. The match had lasted for less than five minutes but I was completely exhausted.

We strutted out of the arena with the crowd still yelling at us. I heard one of the commentators saying, "I know some male wrestlers who would be a little reluctant to get into the ring with Mad Maxine."

Back in the dressing room, I sat down and tried to catch my breath. "You've got to remember to hook your opponent's leg when you cover them," Moolah said. I thought I'd done that. Oh shit.

"And you've got to vary the speed of the match. Sometimes you go fast and sometimes you have to slow it down and catch your breath. That way you don't get so blown up. Know what I mean?"

She looked over at me but my eyelids were heavy. The adrenaline was leaving my system and all I wanted to do was sleep. She stood in front of me.

"I'll take the cash now," she said. I tried to take off a boot but it was stuck. I lifted my boot to pull it off and she just scoffed. At the doorway, she called one of the men to come in and do the honors. He pulled it off and 10 damp hundred-dollar bills scattered on the floor. I saw him calculating whether he could grab one, but then he glanced over at Moolah and left. I handed the bills to her, wrapped in a paper towel.

"Man, I'm glad that's over," I said, heading to the shower.

"That wasn't a bad first match," she said. "The one tonight will be even better."

I thought she was joking so I laughed. I looked at her when she didn't join in.

"Nobody said anything about a second match," I said.

"Consider it part of your initiation into the club," she said. "Go ahead and shower and we'll go to the hotel for a rest. The match isn't until midnight. It's in Brooklyn so we need to leave by 10."

I didn't even say good-bye when we got to the hotel at 4. I set a wakeup call for 6:30 and collapsed on the bed.

Chapter 35

MANGLING MAIM

N o matter how many times I asked her, Moolah refused to tell me where we were going.

"What difference does it make?" she said. "All you need to know is that you'll earn an extra $50 for a few minutes work. These are hardcore wrestling fans. You're going to love it."

We pulled into the parking lot of Biggs Boxing Gym, a nondescript cinderblock building. The stink hit me like an old jockstrap to the face but, after a while, I stopped noticing it.

An older man with a comb-over and mashed nose was telling a couple of younger men where to place the folding chairs. Moolah had already gone into the office, so I stopped to ask him a few questions.

"The big money people get the chairs," he said. "We set out three rows and everyone else stands."

"How much are tickets?" I asked.

"It's $500 for a seat and a hundred clams for standing room," he said. I blanched. Did Moolah want to pay me $50 with those ticket prices?

"So what's it like?" I asked. "This is my first time."

"Your boss ain't told you what this is all about?" he asked. I shook my head.

"It's not really my place," he said and started walking away.

"Can't you help me out? I'm coming in blind."

He turned back around and looked at me. He scanned the room for eavesdroppers and said, "It's loud and people do not always behave themselves."

Frowning, Moolah waved me over from an office doorway and handed me a key.

"There's a locker room down the hall on the left. Get dressed," she said. "Some folks want to meet you before the match."

I shook out my still-damp unitard and put it on. I teased my hair to an upright position. I was finishing up my war paint when Moolah knocked on the door.

"Ready or not, it's time." I didn't have anywhere to keep the key so I handed it back to her.

Men were queuing outside the front doors. A bunch of high rollers massed at the far end of the gym. They grabbed at the gallon bottles of cheap booze lining a folding table. Moolah, in her sequined jacket, waded into the mass. More than once, I swatted someone's hand off my ass and found a wall to lean against to prevent other unwelcome gropes.

"So, fellas, this is my new protégé, Mad Maxine. She had her first match today and did all right. But, we all know the real test is how she does tonight."

There were some chuckles and sounds of agreement among the men. My heart started beating faster.

"She's going up against Mangling Maim tonight," Moolah said. The murmurs turned into whispers, some of the fans shaking their heads.

Another woman wrestler joined the reception. There was no mistaking her. Muscles rippled under a bright red bathing suit and she had a body builder's rolling walk. They moved out of her way, not daring to paw her as they had me.

She ignored them and strode over, holding my eyes in an intense look. Instead of the wimpy wrestlers' shake I'd expected, she crushed my hand. I returned the pressure at first but it soon grew too painful.

She let go only when Moolah quietly told her, "Okay, that's enough."

"I'm going to have fun tonight," she said to me. Swinging her attention to the crowd, she said, "Anyone think I can't take her?" Quick as a snake, she slapped me hard on the face and turned her back to me. She took a gamble that I wouldn't come after her. In shock, I held my burning cheek and felt my temper rise.

The men, who'd been watching me closely, refilled their drinks and headed to their seats. By now the doors were open and the newcomers were finding their places behind the chairs.

"Showtime," Moolah said to me, leading me to the ring. I jumped up and down to test its flexibility but there was no give.

"It's a boxing ring," Moolah said. "There's no give so bumps are going to hurt a little more."

A tuxedoed gent climbed into the ring to announce the first match.

"In this corner," he said, gesturing to me, "Is Mad Maxine, an Amazon of giant proportions. She's the newest addition to the Fabulous Moolah's stable of strong and sexy lady wrestlers. She's here to kick ass and take names."

"Go strut your stuff," Moolah said, pushing me forward. The crowd thundered its approval and, despite my tiredness and terror, I got a warm feeling.

Maim glared at me from the far turnbuckle, her arms stretched out along the ropes. When the announcer turned toward her, she jumped up on the second rope, facing the crowd. She held her arms up in a gesture of triumph.

"And in this corner," he continued, "Is Mangling Maim, champeen of the underground wrestling world. Undefeated in the last two years, she's ready to rumble." She bounced off the ropes and strutted around the ring. Near my corner, she did a head fake and I flinched. The announcer climbed out of the ring and, two seconds later, the bell rang.

"You've got to let her cut you," the Fabulous Moolah said, her whiskey voice almost drowned out by the men's howl. Speaking directly into my ear, she repeated, "She's going to juice you." It took a few seconds to register that she wanted me to let my opponent, Maim, razor my forehead. Now I understood why she hadn't told me anything before the match; she knew I wouldn't comply.

"She won't hurt you," Moolah said. "Then you're going to take the fall."

There wasn't time to think. Moolah shoved me toward the woman in the middle of the ring. Maim came at me like a missile and we locked arms. She shoved me into a headlock, almost a chokehold. It was hard to breathe. I slapped her waist, the signal to go easy, but she tightened her grip instead. The corners of my eyes started to grey. Adrenaline kicked in. I had to do something before I blacked out.

Instead of pulling away from her, I leaned in and punched her hard as I could in the crotch. She lost her grip and dropped to her knees. The spectators bellowed for more. I should've pressed the advantage but I wanted to get away. I stumbled back to the turnbuckle and Moolah.

"She's hurting me," I told her. "She's not working, she's shooting." I coughed and spit outside the ring. A balding man stepped back to avoid getting hit but not before I caught the salacious look on his face.

"She ain't shooting," Moolah said. "You get through this and you're one of us. You'll be a real lady wrestler. But she's got to juice you."

I was thinking, "no way in hell" when the bell rang and she shoved me toward the ring. Before I could make a plan, she had me in another headlock, her grip even tighter than before. Goddammit, how'd she done that so fast? I pulled back to punch her again when I felt the scrape of a fingernail across my forehead. Then I felt the pain because it hadn't been her fingernail. She'd gouged me with a razor that she'd hidden in the tape around a finger. A curtain of blood gushed down my forehead, blinding me. I wiped my eyes but the blood kept flowing. I reached out blindly for the ropes. I called for Moolah, but she didn't answer.

This was more than I'd bargained for when I began training with the Fabulous Moolah nine months ago. This wasn't play-acting; this was survival. Moolah'd told me to let her win the match but I'd be damned if that was going to happen now. I snatched the rag offered up by one of the fans, tied it tight around my forehead, and stomped back to the center of the ring. Maim was going down.

I turned back to the ring and she was charging me. I pushed away from the corner right before Maim would have slammed into me. I grabbed a handful of black hair and slammed her face into the turnbuckle once, twice, three times. Bang, bang, bang. Stunned, she fell backward. I wasn't going to lose my lead this time. I jumped on top of her chest, pinning her arms with my legs. She tried to kick out but I wasn't going anywhere. I hammered her face, splitting her cheek open. Now we were both bleeding and that made me feel just a little better. Moolah yelled at me from the corner.

"You got to let her get UP, Max."

I shot her a look like "don't you dare." Maim took advantage of my momentary diversion and kicked one more time. This time, she dislodged me and sprang to her feet. I swiped at the sweat mixed with blood that dripped into my eyes, the rag now totally saturated. We both panted.

From a low wrestler's crouch, we came at each other like jackhammers. She went for a headlock but I knew this trick and resisted. Instead, I put her into a headlock and raked her eyes along the top rope while she screamed. I threw her into the ropes.

Partly blinded, she sprang back toward me and I was ready to clothesline her. But she ducked under my arm and drop-kicked me hard in the chest. I stumbled backward but kept on my feet. The ring was like concrete and I wasn't going to go down if I could avoid it. She came at me with another dropkick and I leaned back so she missed me by a couple of inches and landed on the boards. A loud thud and she lay gasping. The breath had been knocked out of her so I threw myself on top of hers and hooked her right leg. The ref counted one, two, victory was so close I could smell it. Moolah reached through the ropes and yanked my mohawk, wrenching my neck back. I hit back at her hands while, from the corner of my eye, I saw Maim fumble to find the razor she'd used on me earlier. She was going to cut my throat if I didn't break Moolah's hold. With all my strength, I lunged backward and caught Moolah's hair and pulled with all my might. A mass of shellacked hair came off in my hands. She screamed and let go. Maim had given up on finding the razor and was frantically climbing up to the top rope.

Inexperienced as I was, I figured she was planning to launch herself on top of me. Just as she was getting ready to stand upright, I sprinted across the ring and threw her up and out toward the middle of the ring. She was air-born and heading for the most painful belly bump of her life. This time, she wasn't getting up and Moolah wasn't interfering. I covered moaning Maim with my body, watching out for Moolah, who started to sidle toward me. The ref smacked the mat and the bell signaled the end of the match.

I took a deep breath and sat back on my haunches, suddenly aware of the deafening sound and angry faces. I hadn't taken the fall as I'd been told. Fuck them, I thought. The ref grabbed my wrist and pulled me up.

The announcer cried, "And the winner of the first bout is Mad Maxine." I was trembling with exhaustion. I headed toward a glowering Moolah and the locker room.

I barely remember the drive to the airport hotel. Moolah didn't talk to me until we reached the parking lot.

"Our flight's at noon so we need to get out of here by 8," she said and walked away.

I set the wakeup call for 6:00 a.m., took a long, hot bath, and fell asleep.

෴

I had finished packing my toothbrush and deodorant when I checked for my return ticket. I'd deliberately put it in the zippered side pocket of my suitcase. I unpacked and repacked it but it wasn't there. I methodically went through the room but after an hour I gave up. I was stumped. I had never lost so much as a bus ticket. And now, when it counted most, I'd managed to lose track of my ticket back to Columbia.

Panicked, I knocked on the adjoining door to Moolah's room. The door opened a crack but I barely recognized her. She was completely free of makeup. No thick foundation, eyeliner, or long false lashes. My shock must've been apparent because she began to push the door closed.

"I'll be down in a little while," she drawled. I put my foot against the door.

"Wait. I can't find my plane ticket." Through a crack in the door, I explained the situation to her.

"You're so careless," she growled. "I guess I'm going to have to buy you a new one. But it's coming out of your pay. I can't afford to pick that up myself."

I went back to my room and sat on the bed. Could she have taken the ticket from my bag? I wrestled with a growing sense of mistrust. Then it struck me, if she stole my ticket, she could charge me for covering the cost of a second one and cash-in the first one. The plan had the advantage of making me feel unsure of myself and putting me in her debt. She was a master manipulator. The more I thought about it, the more I was sure she'd taken it.

Chapter 36

SHOWDOWN AT
CAMP MOOLAH

Neither of us said a word on the flight or the drive home from the airport. I was disillusioned and sore. Blood seeped from the cut on my forehead seep. After paying for my lost ticket, I barely earned anything.

As we neared Moolah Drive, I began worrying if the red pickup would be there. But it was gone. It was exactly three in the afternoon when we turned left onto the property. Moolah parked her fat Caddie in the driveway, slammed the door, and headed to her house without a word.

Did she expect me to bring in her bag? The hell with that. I hauled out my duffel and stomped home. I was halfway down the road, when Giselle and Billie ran up.

"You're not going to believe what happened," Giselle said, hyperventilating.

"Moolah sent Brandy out to that pervert," she said, her voice shaking. "She's only 16 years old and that bitch sent her out there. Just like she did to me."

Billie put her hand on Giselle's arm. "We should talk about this inside," she said quietly. "We don't need anyone reporting back to the big house. My god, Max. What happened to your face?" In addition to the deep cut in my forehead, my left eyelid was almost swollen shut.

"Moolah screwed me big time," I said. "Tell you later."

By now we were at my place. I unlocked the door and threw my bag inside. Nobody sat down.

"When did she leave? How'd she get to the airport?" I had to process what had happened and what we should do about it.

"We think she left early this morning," Giselle said. "I went by her place after first practice. She never showed up and Wanda didn't know where she was either. I bet she went so she could earn money for our trip."

I felt sick. None of us would have wanted Brandy to earn money this way.

"Moolah set this up before you left for your match," Billie said. "She must know that we're getting ready to leave. That we wouldn't leave without Brandy."

"Yeah, and we're on lockdown. Nobody's allowed to leave camp without her permission. She made Crystal block the back road with her car so we can't get out the back way."

"Okay, let's think about this," I said. "We have the pictures— you picked those up, right, Giselle?" She nodded. "We have traveling money, minus the money I should've gotten from the match." They looked at me quizzically. "Tell you later. We should pack up and leave tonight, after dark. Instead of Miami, we should drive straight to Albuquerque and get Brandy. We'll put the fear of the goddess into that goddamn pervert."

Giselle looked at me like I was stupid. "Didn't you hear what I said? We can't get out."

"I'm willing to bet that Crystal will move the car if we ask her," I said. "We'll need to create a diversion so no one sees us leave."

I put my hand, palm down, in the middle of the table, and

waited. Half a second later Giselle covered my hand with hers, then Billie joined us.

"Let's do it," Billie shouted and we threw our hands in the air like some deranged softball team.

I grabbed three glasses and pulled cold tea from the fridge. While my back was turned, I opened the silverware drawer and reached far into the back. I pulled out Walter's business card. An idea was percolating.

"I know how to create a distraction," I said. "Leave it to me. When it happens, they won't be thinking about us. Just pack your car. Keep it quiet. Giselle, pull your car near your front door so you can load it without them seeing. Billie can act as look-out."

"What about Brandy's stuff?" Giselle asked. "Shouldn't we bring it with us?"

"Talk to Wanda," Billie said. "Tell her what Moolah's done. She's going to be pissed that Moolah pimped out Brandy and I'm pretty sure she's not a spy." I nodded.

"I'll map our route and pull together road food," I said, remembering the road atlas I'd picked up.

I called Dave when they left. It was his day off, so I thought I might catch him. He picked up after seven rings. His dog Mack barked in the background.

"I have a really big, weird favor to ask," I said. "I want you to call up the local Klan Titan. His name is Walter. Tell him you know the address of that tall, freelance journalist who wrote the Klan story for the Black News and then give him Moolah's address. I made him look like a racist idiot in the article, which he is. It probably wasn't great for his car business." I heard him exhale.

"Pippi, this is a terrible idea," Dave said. "They're going to come after you and then what're you going to do? You can't wrestle someone with a gun."

"I need a diversion. We've got to leave town and it's the only way. There's a lot of shit going down. I wouldn't ask if it wasn't important. Please, help us."

There was a long pause. I wasn't sure he'd do it.

"Okay, give me the number. But for the record, I think you're crazy," he said. "Is there anything else I can do?"

I thought about it. If the Klansmen were true to character, they'd be firing up a cross on Moolah's lawn by nightfall. It might be good to have witnesses.

"Would you call Merl at GROW and Tyrell at the Black News and tell them what's going on? Call Ron and Raquel too. Tell everyone to bring their cameras. I want to make sure those Klan creeps are caught in the act." I gave him the phone numbers.

When I hung up, I realized that I'd just asked Dave for a major favor and quit my job. I hated abandoning him but there was no way around it.

I spent the next hour making quick decisions on what to bring. My new wrestling gear, the orange flokati rug, the pearl diver painting, my books, camera, and toothbrush. Not much. Billie dragged her stuff over in Hefty bags. We had no problem jamming everything in my Plymouth Volare's roomy trunk.

I called Keith's answering machine. I'd promised to meet him at the hospital but that wasn't possible now. I had to tell him I was leaving. I imagined him returning home to an empty house and checking his messages. I had to be tender and thoughtful.

"Keith, sweetie, I hope your father's on the mend. You and your family have been in my thoughts constantly. I'm praying that his condition has improved. I'm sorry not to be able to join you at the hospital. I feel terrible about that. I'm leaving you this message because a lot has happened since you've been gone. The Klan is coming after me because of the Black News article and I have to get out of Dodge. I'll call you from the road. Please don't worry. Billie and Giselle are with me."

Brandy and Wanda's barrack was the last stop. I knocked lightly and Wanda answered the door, eating a Ho-Ho. "Where's Brandy?" she asked.

"I can't tell you exactly what's going on except that Moolah sent Brandy to a pervert in Albuquerque," I said. "We're going to go get her. I'm here for her stuff. Please don't tell anyone. You must say you don't know anything. Okay?" She nodded.

She led me into Brandy's room. I jammed her clothes and heavy metal music cassettes into a garbage bag. The light was fading fast. I hauled Brandy's stuff to Giselle's car. For once, luck was on our side because none of the old faces were anywhere to be seen.

It was getting late. Those Klan assholes were on their way. I could sense them coming closer as the minutes passed. In the fading light, we finished loading Giselle's car. She closed her trailer door for the last time.

"You were a good home to me," she said, patting the pink trailer. She looked at me. "Ready?"

She drove us over the lake road and parked behind my duplex, right next to my car. We stood on the porch for a moment.

"We've got to get Billie and go," Giselle said. "There's not much time."

The sunset was beautiful. A pink and gold band of light hovered through the trees. My reverie was interrupted by barking dogs. Across the lake, I saw a shadowy figure throw something over the fence and the barking abruptly stopped. My guess was Moolah's mutts were busy wolfing up hamburger laced with sleeping pills.

I made one last phone call to Officer Earle. I told him something bad was about to happen at Moolah's.

"What do you mean, 'Something bad is going to happen?' " he pressed.

"There were more of those Klan creeps around the gate this afternoon," I lied. "Someone just came on the property and now the dogs aren't barking. It's bad. Somebody's going to get hurt. Or killed. Please send a patrol car." He was in the middle of a sentence when I hung up.

Billie crashed through the door. "Something's going on at Moolah's!" she said. We ran to the porch and saw men in white robes running across Moolah's lawn. They were carrying a six-foot-tall wooden cross in the direction of the flag pole. Around the lake, porch lights started switching on.

Shrieks carried out over the water. By now it was too dark to tell whether Moolah was yelling at the Klan or the Klan yelling at Moolah. The cross was in flames, shooting higher as the breeze picked up. Sparks floated toward the big house. The dogs still weren't barking. We were under siege. Wolfgang and Crystal argued on their front porch. He pushed her away and went inside. When he returned, he was carrying his shotgun.

I called over to him. "Don't go over there, Wolfgang. The cops are coming, and you don't want to get caught in the middle of this." Crystal tried to pull him inside.

Flames brightened the sky. Something besides the cross had caught fire. Wolfgang shook her off and ran toward the blaze. Moolah's house was on fire and the flames were spreading. Crystal ran after Wolfgang, but I cut her off.

"I need to move your car, Crystal. Please. Where are your keys?"

She frowned at me, trying to grasp the situation but there was no time. Wolfgang was halfway down the lake road. She made a split-second decision and threw her keys to me. I fought an almost physical desire to follow them.

I looked back at Billie and Giselle, who were paralyzed on my front porch. Their eyes were wide and frightened but they also looked determined.

"Let's get the fuck out of here," I said.

I moved Crystal's car just enough to slide by and left her key in the ignition. I hopped in my car and Billie joined Giselle in hers. We closed the doors gently. We rolled without headlights slowly down the dirt road. Right before we hit the pavement, I braked to make sure the coast was clear. It was a good thing I hesitated. Two police cruisers barreled down the street with their cherries flashing. I hesitated another moment and saw Merl, Dave, and my other pals from GROW in one car. Tyrell and Charles followed closely behind in a sleek black sedan. Last, were Ron and Raquel who zoomed past us on a motorcycle. They were all here to bear witness. Whatever happened tonight was going to be published, photographed, and discussed. No more cowardly nighttime escapades, no more cover-of-darkness Klan crap.

They hung a left onto Moolah Drive and we peeled right. We headed for the highway. With a lot of help, we had sicced these assholes on each other. Next stop: Albuquerque.

Chapter 37

ALBUQUERQUE IN OUR SIGHTS

We streaked through Augusta, Georgia, and kept going. We stopped five hours later somewhere outside of Birmingham, Alabama. My tank was on empty and my bladder was on full. I ran for the ladies and, afterward, grabbed hotdogs, cokes, and chips.

Standing in the Gas-n-Go checkout line, I could see that Giselle had been crying. Her eyes were swollen and she kept taking these hiccupy breaths. Billie had her arm around her waist, pretty much holding her up. Two men in gimme hats stared at us so we paid for our snacks and got out of there fast.

"Is she okay?" I asked Billie.

"That night with Howie was the worst thing that ever happened to her," Billie said quietly, "and I think she's reliving it. She needs time to realize that she's safe. I'll take care of her."

"I know you will," I said. "She's lucky to have you. If she's up to it, maybe she can tell us what she wants us to do to the perv once we get there. I have some ideas but she's the one he hurt. She should have a say in it."

I turned back to the atlas on the hot hood of my car. I ran a finger along our route, running east to west.

"It's about 18 more hours to Albuquerque," I said. "We're making good time but we shouldn't stop anywhere for more than 10 minutes."

Billie and Giselle nodded. We were on a rescue mission. We had to try to get to Albuquerque before Howie hurt Brandy, but that was a long shot. Billie and Giselle got back in the car. Giselle laid her head on Billie's lap and fell asleep.

Billie merged onto the highway and found a trucker going 85. I tucked behind her and we rode his tailwind for 100 miles. After he peeled off, we found another trucker and did the same thing. I started thinking of truckers as road angels.

I wasn't sleepy. I didn't even want to listen to the radio, not that there was much in the way of choice. Christian shows and country music.

I was glad to be alone. It gave me time to think and breathe. It felt like we'd busted out of jail. Joy and gratitude flooded me as I thought about all the people who'd come to help us. They'd known me less than a year but when I called, they'd come running.

I wondered if the Black News would run a story about the Camp Moolah cross burning. I regretted not being the one to write it. I wondered if the North Carolina assholes would gain a toehold or would the Columbians fend them off? Would the cops arrest the Klan idiots?

I thought about Keith and how sweet he'd been to me. I hoped his dad would recuperate. My heart ached a little. He and I had had a real connection, and if I were at a different stage in my life, we might've lasted. I replayed scenes from our time together as if I was watching a movie. Our meeting at Group Therapy, our first kiss, the superman underwear, the bone-cracking hugs that made me feel whole.

We drove through the night and the next day, taking

short breaks in Arkansas and Oklahoma and Texas. We only stopped long enough to pee, splash water on our faces, and buy wrinkled red-hots that had spent too long in the rotisserie. We popped No-Doz pills like candy.

Giselle slowly came back to life. She shook off her despair and took a turn at the wheel. Billie grabbed a few hours of shut-eye and then I took a turn.

With each stop, we honed our plan. What it lacked in finesse, it made up for in brute force. Sometimes a sledgehammer is what it takes, Giselle said. Near the New Mexico border, we made a quick detour to pick up duct tape and garbage bags.

It was 8 p.m. when we arrived at Howie's fancy spread. A rustic ranch sign hung over the driveway entrance on our way to the sprawling one-story house. Lucky for us, lights from the nearest neighbors were at least 20 miles away.

I banged on the perv's door. We waited a few minutes but no answer. I pounded again and didn't let up. After a while, I heard muttering on the other side but still no answer. I was getting ready to knock on the door again when it opened a crack. That's all we needed. We pushed through into the house, toppling the little man backward.

Before he'd hit the ground, Billie and Giselle had grabbed him under his arms and pulled him into the house backward on his heels. He wore a maroon satin robe over matching boxers. His robe, a size too small, barely covered his furry paunch. Spindly legs like ice cream parlor chairs stuck out below.

"What are you doing?" he screamed. "Get out of my house or I'm calling the police. Stop this!" He spoke like someone used to giving orders. I slapped a piece of duct tape over his mouth. Shocked, his eyes bulged and his face turned red. He had no clue the trouble he was in. Three righteously pissed-off lady wrestlers had just invaded his home.

Billie and Giselle shoved him hard into a chair and held him still as I taped his arms and ankles to it. For extra security, I taped the chair to a side table. He was going nowhere. He mumble-screamed into the tape, his face purpling.

"Calm the fuck down," I said, checking my watch. It had taken only minutes to disable him. From this moment forward, his life would change. We were in charge.

Taking over his house was the first step. Next was finding Brandy. Giselle bolted for the back of the house, running toward the room with the pink-canopied bed. Billie and I were close on her heels. She ran down a long hall, stopping at a door near the end. She put her open hand on the wall and bent her head as if praying or passing out. She looked back at us, eyes filled with tears.

"I can't," Giselle said. She was close to losing it.

Billie pulled her close into a tight hug. I slid past them into the room. I felt for the light switch and turned on the overhead. There it was, the pink monstrosity, the princess nightmare. But Brandy wasn't in it.

"Check the bathroom," Giselle said, pointing to the left of the bed.

"Brandy? Brandy, are you there?" I waited but didn't hear anything. I knocked again. "Brandy, honey, open up. You're safe now." I heard murmuring. "Brandy! It's us. We're getting you out. Brandy, answer me."

I checked the lock. It was like the one I'd had on my bedroom door when I was a kid so I knew how to pick it. I flipped the top plate off and popped it open.

Brandy was across the room, squeezed behind the toilet. Her head rested on the seat, her eyes facing the wall. All she wore was a towel around her waist, her huge breast squashed behind the toilet. I squatted next to her but she didn't stir. I reach over and touched her shoulder.

"Brandy, are you hurt? Talk to me." Slowly, she lifted her head. A bruise discolored her cheek and her eyes were swollen. She didn't speak.

"Let's get you out of here," I said, trying to raise her by the arms. I couldn't do it by myself so I called for Billie who was still in the hallway with Giselle. They entered the bathroom.

"No!" Giselle screamed and rushed toward Brandy. She knelt and threw her arms around the injured girl. Brandy was still limp but registered her presence. She leaned into Giselle and sobbed.

Billie and I silently agreed to give them a few minutes. I looked around the bathroom. Brandy's yellow wrestling suit was lying on the floor near the bath. One of the straps was broken.

At my signal, Billie and I guided them up as a single unit and walked them into the bedroom. Giselle pulled Brandy on to the bed and held her like a child. They rocked back and forth while Giselle hummed.

"It's going to be all right. We're here now. You're going to be okay," Giselle kept telling her.

Brandy cried for a long time. I got her some water and, after a sip, she began telling us what had happened. She, like Giselle, had thought that visiting the perv would be easy money.

"Moolah promised that he only wanted to take photos," Brandy said. "I thought I could earn money for Florida. I was afraid you'd leave me behind." My stomach churned.

"I should've told you what he did to me," Giselle murmured into her hair. "It's my fault. I should've told you." Billie sat down on the bed next to Giselle.

"It's not your fault," Billie said in a firm voice. "It's that asshole's fault and nobody else's." Giselle blinked and then nodded. Brandy continued her story.

He had picked her up from the airport and taken her out for a steak dinner. She drank a little too much wine. Then he drove her out to his house.

"I was tired and wanted to go to sleep but he told me to suit up so we could make some movies. It was cool at first. He was looking through the lens and telling me how beautiful I am," she said, wiping her nose. "Then he got all hot and freaky."

He wrestled her to the ground, ignoring her pleas to stop. He'd slapped her and called her a slut. He pulled her hair and made her follow him around the room as if they were in a wrestling match. He threw her to the floor and pinned her. He shoved aside the bottom of her bathing suit and raped her.

"The thing is, it was my first time," Brandy said, burying her head in a pillow. "I know I told you I'd already done it but I was lying. I didn't want to be a virgin but I didn't want it to happen like this." She started crying again.

None of us said anything. This was so much worse than we'd expected.

"Brandy, I know you've been through a lot, but you have a decision to make," I said. "Do you want to go to the hospital and report the rape? They would want to swab you for semen. They'd also check for trauma and ask you some questions."

Brandy was silent. My heart thumped in my neck.

Billie scoffed. "Who are you kidding? He's a doctor and she's a nobody. They're not going to believe her."

"You're probably right. The other option is to punish him ourselves," I said, nodding to the living room. "It's lucky, we've got that scumbag tied up in the living room."

Brandy sat straight up. "He's tied up right now?" she said in a squeaky voice. She went from a hollowed-out shell to a live bomb in seconds. She launched off the bed and ran to the living room. The perv was right where we left him, struggling to free himself.

"You fucking fucker!" she screamed in his face. Then she punched him so hard his head snapped back. He widened his eyes and tried to say something. She hit him again.

"You like that? Hunh? How about some more?" She let fly with another crack on the side of his head. "Come on, beg for it. Isn't that what you told me?" She smacked both ears at the same time and he screamed behind his gag. "Hurts like a bitch, don't it?"

Giselle walked up behind me, her face drained of color.

"How about you, Giselle?" I asked. "You want a turn?" She looked at Billie, who nodded.

And that's how it went. First Brandy, then Giselle punched and slapped him. Before long, blood streamed from his nostrils and his eyelids began to swell just like Brandy's. He whimpered at every raised hand, but I hardened my heart. This guy had hurt my friends and it was payback time. I didn't necessarily want to see him dead but he deserved an ass-whooping. These were the right women for the job. I turned on the radio to a rock and roll station. They started smacking him in time to Elvis Presley's "You ain't nothing but a hound dog."

They stopped after a while, panting. Beating somebody up is surprisingly tiring, I guess. I took advantage of the pause to open a bottle of Dom Perignon that I'd found in the back of the fridge. It was expensive champagne, meant for a big occasion. I figured this qualified. We shut the door to the living room where Howie slumped in the chair and made ourselves comfortable in the kitchen.

We were starving by the time we finished the bottle. Billie raided the fridge for bread, cheese, and salami and everyone but Brandy ate like it was their last supper. With our mouths full, we weren't thinking about what we'd done or what we'd do next.

At breaks in the music, we could hear labored breathing from the living room. Blood had clotted in his nose, making it hard for him to breathe. I walked over to where he sat in the stink of his misery.

"I'll make it easier for you to breathe," I said. "But you are not permitted to talk. Only the women talk." I paused for emphasis. "One. Single. Word. And I'll tape you again. You understand?"

Asphyxia appeared to be setting in, but he closed his eyes and nodded. I ripped the tape away from his mouth and he took big gulping breaths. I brought him a glass of tap water and held it while he drank. Half of it dribbled down his shirt. He looked at me, his eyes pleading. I walked back to my friends.

"This is pretty good stuff," Giselle said, holding up her champagne. "Is there more?"

"Probably," I said. "We can take a look. I bet he's got a nice wine collection stashed somewhere too. But I need to sleep. How about you all? Tired?"

The wine had done its work and I was barely holding my eyes open.

"You mean we're not leaving?" Brandy protested. "I want to get out of here!"

Giselle was able to persuade her that, in all likelihood, Howie had cleared his schedule to spend 'quality time' with her. There would be no interruptions from the outside world. We desperately needed sleep before we set out again.

"You're safe, honey. No one's going to bother you," she said. Brandy reluctantly agreed to stay another night as long as she didn't have to sleep in the hideous pink boudoir.

We divvied up the bedrooms. Billie and Giselle slept in the master. Brandy took another guest bedroom and I ended up in the dreaded pink room.

It was a mess. I wiped up the blood in the bathroom and threw Brandy's towel in a closet. I took a long hot bath to soothe the aches from my body. By the time I crawled into bed, I could barely keep my eyes open. I turned out the lights and slept hard.

No one else was awake when I got up at six the next morning. I called Connie to let her know that we'd left South Carolina.

"There's a whole lot of weird shit going on," I said. "I'll tell you about it later but I was wondering if we could crash with you on our way to Miami. It'll be four of us."

"Course, hon. I've got plenty of floor space. Your friends are my friends."

That settled, I padded back to where the perv was sitting. He hung his head, urine puddled around him.

"I know I'm not supposed to talk but I'm really sore from sitting like this. Can I lie down? I'm getting bad cramps." I growled at his infraction.

"You're staying in the chair but I guess I can tilt it so you're on your back." I rearranged the chair and he was sleeping by the time I headed back to the kitchen.

It was breakfast time. I found the biggest pan and started frying up bacon. I chopped and sautéed onions and green peppers and scrambled a huge pile of eggs. I toasted a stack of bread and put out butter and jam. The smell of bacon, better than an alarm clock, wafted through the house.

Within 10 minutes, everyone was sitting around the table scarfing down eggs and toasting each other with mimosas.

Giselle downed hers and held her glass out for a refill. She took a healthy sip and set down her glass.

"Any idea where he keeps his wrestling porn?" Giselle asked Brandy.

"Yeah, he keeps that stuff in his study," she said. "When I first got here, he showed me his collection, said I should be proud to be part of it. I should've run away right then."

"Okay, so we grab his nasty stash and then what?" Billie said. She had her arm laid across the back of Giselle's chair.

"We should kill the fucker," Brandy suggested. "Or at least cut his dick off."

"I don't know about you but I don't want to go to prison," Billie said. "I just want to make sure he never hurts anyone again."

"We could make him sign a confession saying that Moolah supplied him underage girls," I said. "If Moolah sends anyone else out here, we could send copies to the police, the American Medical Association, and the newspapers." I looked to see if Brandy and Giselle were going for this.

"His reputation would be shot. He might have his license revoked. And ...," I paused for dramatic effect, "Moolah and he could go to jail for raping and pimping, or spend beaucoup bucks trying to get out of it."

"Okay, so let's get his tapes," Billie said, rising from the table. The phone rang and a familiar voice came through the answering machine. Dizzy, I steadied myself.

"Hi Howie, it's Moolah, calling to see how things are working out with Brandy. I would have called sooner but I had a little house fire to deal with. Nothing for you to worry about. Call me when you get a chance."

I looked at the others. They were frozen, staring at the phone. "It's okay. She doesn't know we're here," I said.

"Over here. The tapes are in here," Brandy said, standing in the door of a room we hadn't explored yet. It was a classic study, with a mammoth wooden desk and bookshelves lining the walls. His oxblood leather furniture and 19th-century horse prints would've looked more at home in Harvard than the rough-and-tumble West.

Brandy pointed to a mahogany cabinet behind the desk. She moved the chair out of the way and tugged on the cabinet handles. No luck. It was locked up tighter than grandma's girdle. She jiggled the handles harder.

"Hold on. I bet the key's around here somewhere," Billie said, scanning the desk.

She found a set of keys in a delicate ceramic bowl and began trying them, one by one. It was the last key on the ring.

The double doors swung open, revealing at least 100 video-tapes labeled by name and date. On the labels in neat script were the biggest names in ladies' wrestling over the last 20 years. The oldest tape was Beautiful Bonita, 1964.

"I know that name! My aunt used to talk about her," Giselle said. "I can't believe he's been at it this long."

We took Bonita's tape out of its cardboard cover and loaded the VCR. The first shot was a close up of a much younger Howie adjusting the camera. His smarmy smile filled the frame until he finished his adjustments and ran back to the woman. All of us groaned when we saw his red speedo. She was short and powerfully built, her eyes outlined in dark kohl. But her dominant feature was a huge afro.

"Groovy, groovy," he said. "Now that you're warmed up, I want to try out some other stuff." He moved closer to her. The audio was muffled. He put his hand on her left hip and she slapped it off.

"What are you doing? Get your fucking hands off of me,"

she said in a Brooklyn accent. His back was to the camera so you couldn't see what was happening. All of a sudden, he pulled back his right hand and slapped her hard.

"You bitch. You knew damn well what was going down."

Giselle had her arm around Brandy. "Some things never change," she said.

He slapped her again and she was down on one knee. She paused and then drove into him like a linebacker. He was down and out of the frame. There was some inaudible noise and he was dragging her back into the frame by her beautiful black hair. He pinned her arms and snarled in her face.

"You think Moolah's going to let you wrestle if you don't do what I want? You'll never get another booking," he rasped. She stared up at him with a look of pure hatred.

A minute passed and the truth of what he'd said sank in. All the fight went out of her. He barked a laugh as though he had won something. He pulled out his penis. She turned her head and she looked right into the camera, sad and broken.

The act lasted no more than 30 seconds, but it was an eternity. I broke out in a sweat and turned away. Giselle shut off the player.

"I'm going to kill that fucking fucker," she whispered. "He's been doing this for years. Me and Brandy were just two more marks."

"Think about it. If we kill him, the cops will figure out Brandy was here," I said. "She'll go to prison, for sure. We have to make sure he doesn't do this again and we don't get caught."

Billie murmured something to her and she seemed to calm down. Brandy, on the other hand, was freaking. What she saw on the tape had just happened to her. It was too fresh. She slid down the wall, her long brown hair completely covering her face.

While they tended to her, I started shoveling the tapes into one of the garbage bags we'd bought. And it wasn't just videos. I'd cleared one row of tapes and saw a row of photo albums. A quick look was all it took to see that they were full of photos of him dominating the wrestlers in one way or another. In many, he was choking the women, in others, he had pinned them so their legs waved in the air. Page after page showed the perv sexually humiliating the women who'd all come out here for an easy payoff. I felt sick.

He kept the negatives in the front of each album. Once we destroyed them, the photos were gone for good. But then it occurred to me that freaks like him probably traded photos. At least this stash would be destroyed. By the time we emptied the cabinet, we had three large bags of tapes and albums. I hauled them to the living room.

"We're taking your porn, dude," I said. "You're lucky we don't burn down your fucking house."

"No!" he said, an involuntary reflex.

At the door, I stopped and stalked back to him.

"There are no excuses for what you've done," I said. "You're a criminal. But I want to know why." I glared at him from four feet away, my fists on my hips.

He started crying. "I'm sick. I can't stop. Please help me."

"Doesn't make a difference what he says," Brandy said. "He did what he did." I looked at Giselle to see what she would say.

"I agree," she said. "We'll take his collection, but I don't think we should kill him ... or burn down his house."

"Thank you," he said quietly, looking at his lap.

A thought occurred to me, "How much did you pay Moolah for each girl?"

"What?" he said, not quite following the conversation. "Oh, I paid her $2,000 for each girl and covered airfare."

"So, Moolah kept $1,500 and gave the girls $500?" It pissed me off, but I wasn't surprised. Just more of the same.

"No, I gave Moolah $2,000 and then I paid the girls $500," he said, too scared to lie.

Goddammit. Moolah was ripping off the girls who paid with their bodies. That fucking asshole.

I went back to his office and typed out a confession for the perv to sign. It said that he had been paying Moolah to send lady wrestlers to him for sexual encounters. I typed out two more statements for Giselle and Brandy, describing what had happened to them and the fact that they were both minors when the rapes occurred.

He signed and dated the confessions. I applied the notary embosser I'd found in his office and he initialed it. Brandy and Giselle both signed as witnesses. I compared his signature to a canceled check I'd found. It was the same.

"I think it'll work. Hold up in court, I mean. I'm also thinking that he should pay Brandy and Giselle damages right now. It'll get us started down in Miami," I said.

We fanned out to look for his safe. We looked behind pictures in the study, but no luck. Maybe it was in his bedroom. We finally found it in his walk-in closet. He had draped an enormous Hermes scarf over it and stacked dress shoes on top.

"We need the combination," I said. "Check his wallet, the desk, any hiding place you can think of."

"Fuck that," Brandy said. "I'll get it out of him."

"Give us the combination to your safe," she said, her arms crossed. He didn't respond right away.

"You don't have a choice," I pointed out. "You give us the

combination and we won't hurt you anymore. If you don't, I can't make any promises."

Brandy stomped on his foot to demonstrate. It got his attention.

"Okay, okay," he said, giving it up. "It's 57 left, 24 right, 10 left."

I put the numbers in and pulled open the heavy door. Bingo. There was at least $20,000 in cash. I grabbed a brick of twenties and passed it to Brandy. I ignored the stocks and bonds. Then I saw the manila folder. I pulled it out and stood up.

"What have we here?" I said, opening the folder. I felt my jaw drop.

There, in black and white, was a much younger Moolah in a headlock. Holding her snug to his waist was a man who resembled Howie. To the side, stood a boy, no older than 12. With identical smiles, father and son were mugging for the camera. The photos underneath showed Howie Senior doing things to a very young Moolah, his son always somewhere in the frame.

I tucked the folder under my arm and we headed to the kitchen. Brandy stacked the money onto the lazy Susan and spun it around.

"That sure is a pretty sight," she said. "More money than I've ever seen in my whole life."

"You and Giselle should keep it," I said. "You're the ones who've been hurt. Maybe it'll take some of the pain away."

Giselle suggested we break it into piles of $5,000 each. "That way we all start even when we get to Miami," she said. Brandy hesitated but then nodded her head.

Once the money had been divvied up, I was ready to leave. "Anyone else want to get the hell out of here?" I said.

The phone rang and we froze.

"Hi, hon. I haven't heard from you and I'm getting a little worried. You may think I'm crazy, but I asked a friend of mine to check in on you. He'll be stopping by in an hour or so."

Crap. Moolah was sending a henchman. It really was time to hit the road.

"We've got to leave now," I said. "We should take some food with us. Giselle, would you make two food bags, one for each car? Grab whatever wine you find. And a corkscrew."

I was going to ask Brandy to help her but she said she needed a quick shower. Billie and I talked over what to do about the perv.

"We should free him," she said, "but we needed some lead time." We agreed to loosen his bonds a little. That way, he could break free after we'd left.

I packed up my toothbrush and made the bed. I thought of all the women who'd trembled in fear under the pink coverlet. The cars were packed and ready to go in half an hour. We were all anxious to leave this bad place.

Brandy was still in the shower when we finished packing. I went in to hurry her along. I could hear crying from the bathroom door. I pulled back the shower curtain and she was sitting motionless, hot water hitting her bowed head. She was having some kind of a delayed response.

"Hold on, honey."

I hollered for Giselle. She knew how to help Brandy through this nightmare better than any of us. I left the bathroom while they talked. She came back out and said, "Brandy's in no shape to leave. She's reliving what happened to her," Giselle explained.

"I don't give a flying fuck if she just had a heart attack," I said. "We have less than half an hour to get out before Moolah's muscle gets here." I was starting to hyperventilate. This was not good.

"Calm down, Pippi," Billie said. "We can figure this out. Can't we pretend like no one's home? Hide our cars until he leaves?"

"No! We have got to leave—now!" I was clenching my fists. Time was running out. I ran back into the bathroom.

"Brandy, I'm sorry. I do care. But we have got to clear out or the shit is going to hit the fan. Now! We've got to get going." She got out of the shower and into some clothes.

Forty-five minutes after Moolah's last call, we were ready. We had just one more task.

"This is it, jerk off. Time to say good-bye. You don't say anything to anyone about us coming here. In fact, you don't answer the door. You got that?"

He nodded and looked up. He moved his eyes from me to Billie, to Giselle, and then to Brandy. I watched him closely and would've slapped him silly if he'd made a wrong move. I was keyed up.

"I'm sorry," he said. "I'm very sorry."

No one said, "that's okay" because it wasn't. It never would be. I cut most of the way through the tape around his wrists and left the tape around his ankles intact. Once we left, he'd be free in 20 minutes. We ran for the cars. Brandy rode with me and Billie piled in with Giselle.

One part of me wanted to head for the hills but I had to know whether the perv would comply with our agreement. I led our mini-convoy up a hill to the east. It had a good view of his house and decent cover. I lay on my belly and peered over the rise.

Less than fifteen minutes later, a car broke the horizon line.

It was a long silver boat of a car, probably a Caddie or a stinkin' Lincoln. It took another 10 minutes for the driver to make it to Howie's driveway. He pulled in and sat there for a couple of minutes.

Finally, he extracted himself from the car. I pulled out my little binoculars and saw him ring the doorbell with a hand as big as a catcher's mitt. "Christ on a bike," Brandy muttered. "He's huge."

We waited to see if Howie would answer. I held my breath. The man walked around to the side of the house away from us. Was he going to break in? I prayed that Howie would lay low. Dear God, please let him keep his yap shut. Please, please, please.

The man-beast came around the other side of the house and looked to the hills. It was like he was looking right at us. I pulled down my binocs to avoid the telltale glint. He pounded on the door again but no answer.

We watched him drive off the same way he'd come, from the west. We waited another 15 minutes to make sure he was really gone. Billie exhaled and it was over.

"Anyone want to go to Miami?" I said.

Brandy let out a loud "yeehaw" and we all started laughing. Like magnets, we moved into a group hug with Brandy in the middle.

"We're going to be okay," I said. "We have plenty of money and a place to stay."

"Yep," Billie said. "I'll call the Florida promoters and see what I can line up. We'll be working in no time."

Giselle looked over at Brandy. "Maybe we should take a couple of weeks to just lie on the beach, drink some pina coladas." Brandy nodded. That sounded pretty good to all of us.

We let ourselves forget about the bag of wrestling porn in

the trunk, the perv, his trashed rancher, and the pimp-queen of wrestling. There was plenty of time to figure out what to do. Maybe we'd return the tapes to the women who'd been forced to star in them. Maybe we'd form a lady wrestler vigilante group. There was plenty of time to figure it out on our way to sunnier climes.

ACKNOWLEDGMENTS

My husband, Steve Hilmy, and my sisters, Marcia Semmes and Carol Mjoseth, might well have feared they'd breathe their last before I completed this book. In my wildest dreams, I never thought it would take 35 years. With their support and encouragement, I finally mustered the courage to type 'The End' and send my baby into the world. A very special thanks to my readers for valuable feedback, including Cara Cobb, Michael Dolan, Jeff Leen, Terri Lewis, Chris Marcum, and Judith Wyatt. I'm also grateful to A.X. Ahmad who led the Writer's Center's advanced fiction seminar and to my fellow writers for their important critiques. Kudos and accolades to the talented David Audet for the cover photo. A giant thank you to Marie Mundaca, the greatest cover designer I could ever imagine. Lastly, I salute the strong and resilient women wrestlers I met at the Fabulous Moolah's training camp. Few understand the sacrifices and risks you took to give the fans matches worth watching. And, of course, bear hugs to the wrestling fans, a more avid and loyal group you will never find.

CPSIA information can be obtained
at www.ICGtesting.com
Printed in the USA
BVHW061322010421
603931BV00009B/763